MOTHERLESS AMERICA:

HOW HISTORY BECAME MUTE

A novella

by

JONATHAN DECOTEAU

The author read and consulted the wonderful book *Gabriel's Rebellion: The Virginia Slave Conspiracies of 1800 and 1802* by Douglas R. Egerton for historical info but strove to devise an original fictional work based on the spirit of Gabriel's rebellion. The author also consulted the text of The U.S Constitution posted by The National Constitution Center but included only text available in the public domain. The author expresses his sincere gratitude to those whose knowledge helped him in the drafting of this book.

Published by Animus Nor Books

eBook ISBN: 979-8-9994196-0-6
Paperback ISBN: 979-8-9994196-1-3

OTHER BOOKS BY THE AUTHOR

Sing of the High Country

A novel-in-stories that looks at the shadow of New England's dark past.

The Naked Earth

The tale of a military criminal seeking redemption for murder in the cities of Iraq.

Bashert

The ghost of a widow's husband returns, seeking to rejoin his love at the cost of her life.

Spree

The spirit of a teen girl killed after driving drunk must save her ex-boyfriend from a school shooting.

The *War of the Animals* Series

The rise and fall of a genetically enhanced animal civilization over ten generations.

Snake City Chronicles

An abused woman who just wanted to have a good date night becomes a vigilante for women's rights.

Yesterday, Today, and Tomorrow

TABLE OF CONTENTS

By directive of The Oracle, races are now extinct. Words like "black" and "white" are hereby erased. Colors will assume new names. Language is dangerous and must be controlled at all times. Original ideas are Armageddon and must be destroyed upon creation. For the greater peace, society shall be postracial. Every skin shall resemble every other skin. Every history of discord shall be erased. For what is history but the great enemy of progress? All must look equally, speak equally, and think equally. In our homogeneity lies our strength.

–From The Oracle's AI Downloads,
the first programs received by The New People
upon The Oracle's Rise.

CHAPTER 1

Terror pulsed in the room like a red power light endlessly blinking. Pungent and palpable, the neurofeeling shot through the wireless Oracle, the very pinnacle of artificial intelligence, to the point that not even the most miniscule microchip in the smallest artificial leaf was immune to a fearsome shudder. The great green sky eye, relentlessly pulsing, communicated to its brother and sister sky eyes that an organic brain wave, free of all artificial enhancements, had created a monstrosity of such epic proportions that the whole Oracle would need to reboot. In a single microsecond, the consumers might feel the radical sensation of a creature not sighted in nearly one-thousand digital years: an original thought. The consumers might see the fruits of its perverse labors: in a single nanosecond, the raised image of a man of color, sinewy hemp lining his soft neck, as his legs danced above white-red faces. Just as quickly as the disturbance appeared, the image grew staticky and pixelated and was gone.

After a full oneteenth second, the sky eyes knew that whoever had generated the anomaly was nowhere to be found on its own neural nets. The police apps searched the nets of the entire consumer base, all the multiverses of the direct sensory Net that could possibly be generated. In a fraction of a second, the situation was clear: something organic, some neurovirus, had entered the wireless and replicated itself at astonishing speed. One image was met with another: there were five-dimensional pictures of people marching, under machine gun fire; another image showed a Cherokee man shot, executed on an open field by passing Union troops. Still another image showed what the machines had coded as The Pacification, the moment when racism was officially cured–or whitewashed–though The Oracle had already eliminated that term. There was also The Pacification's sister act, The Truth Act, the moment when all false narratives, including the radical myth that white people, as one brand of consumer was once called, had enslaved black people, creating an oppressive historical dichotomy of epic proportions, were declared void and eliminated from The Oracle altogether.

To learn history is to repeat it, The Great Green Eye assured the consumers, and so, history was no more. And the consumers, incapable of thinking–or *deviatitis* as the disease, much like tuberculosis, was once called–were inclined to agree. History had too many wounds. It was a thing most warty, most pus-filled and most dirty. And memory, the mother sow of history, rolled around in the same mud and attracted the same fleas. It was easier to forget. To start over. To forge a new five-dimensional reality that stretched back into Time Memory and erased it, replacing what once passed as the historical narrative of the day with images of OnePeople, so that no one was white or black or Cherokee or Haitian or Chinese or anything else that ended with *ese* or *ck* or *te* or other objectionable letters. After all, as the great thinking machines computed, *everything is offensive.* Every statue fell. Every sticking point of history disappeared. Every conversation—which failed to generate greater understanding anyway—fell silent at the same time. There was no need for something as many-legged as a thought, like an especially engorged burrowing tick, to upset the tall green grasses of the Elysian fields of the new peace. There was only the comforting *Om* of the blinking red light.

And now there was this.

Once upon a time, an art history professor, pointing to a work by Claude Monet with one finger and a work by Gerard Sekoto with another, looked out at his class and said, *Most people never have one original thought in their entire lifetimes.* Lacking originality of thought himself, he never knew how profoundly right he was.

The Oracle, the pinnacle in AI consciousness, lived to see it each day. Lack of thought was the great underpinning of humanity, almost like a new inalienable right. A man might rise, might decide it was time to get out of bed and brush his teeth because society conditioned it into him. A woman might undertake a certain job to work for imaginary numbers–nothing tangible, really–that might tell her that she had enough capital to pay her bills. This woman might rise and make sure her kids got up for school because she had habitually undertaken the task without thought. Society had simply conditioned gender norms into her. And for however many intellectuals stirred the great melting pot of homogeneity, there were far more that never heard their words. The thinkers of societies grew more and more removed from the people. And so, the masses of humanity plodded on, subjected to a servitude to the machine that they'd never be cognizant enough to understand. Books like *Fahrenheit 451* and movies like *The Matrix* attempted to show them their realities. For a moment, people would grapple with the profound ideas, talk them out, process them. But then that moment would be gone and it would be time for the next entertainment, the next *TikTok* video, the next Netflix series. The wonders of the universe, of a multiverse, really, lay like treasures in the speckled cosmos awaiting discovery, yet most never looked past the surfaces of their cell phones to see the sky.

Such a complacency of convenience appeased The Oracle. Directives like Preserve The Peace, Whatever The Cost, were drilled into the machine's code by inventors whose names were hidden by a collective corporate identity. And so, The Oracle controlled the weather, the flow of commerce, the rise of technology, and the thoughts of the human brain. Everyone was connected to live feed at their births, and even their thoughts were machine-rendered. Organics were augmented as babies, imbibing files as they aged, connected to a ubiquitous mainframe. And then they began lives devoid of purpose, but plush with apathy. The man or woman or organic noted earlier would move to machine-controlled labor. While some helped service the hardware of The Oracle, The Oracle was largely self-sufficient. And so, the men and women elected to recreate. They would visit digital museums, play digital games, partake in fake wars, in one sweepingly gamified Metaversal reality. Constant brain flow with The Oracle lessened as time went on, as The Oracle started to think for humans.

Almost instantaneously, The Oracle worked on achieving its directive, erasing history, race, words, cultures, heritages in the blink of a cursor. No one thought enough to care, and so no one intervened. Occasional aberrations existed. A Sojourner Truth might be reborn, but she was quickly snuffed out. A Martin Luther King, Jr. might dream, but The Oracle could easily change the parameters of the dream to make sure it was full of lively red, whites, and blues, and that it lived and died with him. A Benjamin Franklin might awaken to trace the currents of electricity only to forget the thought.

The Oracle was masterful at suppressing those who hadn't the slightest idea they were suppressed, since they hadn't the slightest idea of anything.

Everyone was free. Peaceful. Happy.

And now, regrettably, there was this.

Artifact 1

From The National Anthem

O say can you see, by the dawn's early light,
What so proudly we hail'd at the twilight's last gleaming
One nation, motherless, fatherless, its future assured,
its past free of meaning?

CHAPTER 2

013686 shuddered the moment history coursed through his veins. His pale white eyes opened, even as he slept in his crude apartment bed, and suddenly, there he was, his mind adrift in the cybertrash of ages. The deleted narratives floated in a sea of sapient light, calling out to his outstretched hands. Entire wars, much like the mythical American Revolution, were confined to eroding files. There was a documentary on African slaves arriving in St. Augustine, Florida in 1565; there was Lincoln delivering the Gettysburg Address; there was Malcolm X saying half-muted phrases like "*You can't separate peace from freedom because no one can be at peace unless he has freedom*" and other unnecessary bits of agitating historical data, like the Declaration of Independence and its vague insinuations about God and "*rights to Life, Liberty, and the Pursuit of Happiness.*" The vast repository of junk files swelled, the data entering into the organic's mind as the files sought to interact with a human interface, the way they were at the elimination of any human-run Internet hundreds of years ago, when many were first designed.

Yet, 013686 spent the night hours downloading even the most corrupted of files, including those of a young Gabriel, slave of Thomas Prosser–when organics were so named–a young blacksmith, who, like 013686, stood over six-feet in height, and had, according to a newspaper article of the time, a bony face said to be symmetrical and well-made, whatever that might mean. Like 013686, Gabriel Prosser possessed a larger physique and was a literate man, yet a fighter, someone capable of drawing blood and igniting fire. Apparently, this Gabriel intended to draw the words "Liberty or Death" on a flag before abducting a prehistoric Governor James Monroe to negotiate for the end of something called slavery in Virginia in 1800. The images of the man, blurred, drew a sense of solidarity from 013686, who declared himself *Gabriel* after the slave revolt leader, whose images he saw, along with twenty-two others, hanging in the gallows. The body swayed in 013686's mind well into the night.

Yet, Gabriel, or The Historian, as he fancied himself, stared at his own skin. He saw that while he might call himself black, in the archaic tongue, generations of post-racial breeding programs left little that might distinguish Gabriel from any other organic. Whatever heritage Gabriel might lay claim to, he couldn't say. It had been washed from his blood by the chemical tide of forgotten history. Yet, Gabriel could feel some kinship with the images of slaves, the probing eyes of Gabriel Prosser, at the core of his soul, something he could not explain but only feel the way a child feels blood first rushing to its suddenly upturned head. Gabriel knew that the blood of men and women, of slaves from ages long since erased, flowed through his own blood, and boiled, blistering the soul. Yet, The Historian could never know for sure–such was the evasive nature of junk file history.

Whatever rebirth Gabriel underwent, he knew that his time was short. The Oracle fed chemicals that would make him forget, that would lull him from sleep into a consciousness where all of the junk files would be deleted. The Historian would have to free himself from the chemical receptors that held him in intellectual bondage. And so, borrowing from the example of his forebear, the blacksmith who fashioned scythes for the day of rebellion, Gabriel cut away at the sensors that held him, anxious to open his eyes after his long night of sleep, anxious to see the first light of the organic world.

Artifact 2

The Pledge of Allegiance

I pledge allegiance to the United States of America, and to the authority for which it stands, one Nation, indivisible, with one common thought for all.

CHAPTER 3

The Militante sat in his augmented desk, an iron chair that allowed him to see into The Oracle for even the least variation in its neural signal. Parts of The Militante had been something of a man, someone or something vaguely human. But those were vestiges of a life of the flesh that the great augmented organic recalled only through a computerized lens. The Militante was the personification of The Oracle's directive now. And like history, its memory was a video stream of unadulterated cries, of bloodshed and murder, a tale told by a digitized idiot, signifying nothing. If The Militante were to describe itself as a man–and a masculine presence was what it currently projected to the stream–it would say that it vaguely resembled an augmented soldier, with huge, multicolored eyes, a broad forehead and jagged cheekbones that somehow funneled down into a narrow, serpentine slit of a mouth. All else fed into the uniform: a sturdy, blood-red vest that resembled more of an homage to the military tyrants of centuries past, as if The Militante's very skin had blood flowing on the outside as well as the inside, from so many kills. Still, there was a meticulousness about the outfit, something computer-generated, nearly like The Militante itself.

"Son of the machine," a voice like metal shards clanging together said. "We have a new case to feed into your neural pathways."

The voice was that of The Oracle, the great calculating AI program of the digital multiverse that governed all possible outcomes of all possible computer models and selected the best outcomes for all.

The Militante nodded. "Show me the latest junk file," it said.

The Oracle obliged. Before The Militante, in holographic mode, stood 013686. The Militante watched as the organic fumbled through long discarded, half-eroded junk files that someone, something had purposely left in a small corner of The Oracle for digital consumers to run into unawares. The Militante searched its neural pathways for any distinguishing sign of who might have planted the files in this brave new augmented reality. There was nothing. The files were perfectly clean of any numbers that might give away their source. Whoever had done this was an expert, perhaps one of the old software engineers that The Oracle had eradicated when it came time for New History to unfold.

Still, the image of the tall, black man searching through the junk files of organic history was a concerning one. It wasn't just the awareness of history. That could be erased and replaced with a New History folder easily enough. It was the natural light in the eyes of this computerized man. There was something more dangerous than knowledge itself brewing in those eyes: an idea, an original one, perhaps the most threatening virus of all.

The Militante knew that nothing caused so much destruction throughout history as the world of ideas. Brilliant women and men, from Sappho to Socrates, from Eve to Jesus of Nazareth, from Franklin to Thoreau to Sontag, had unsettled the world with radical ideas. Some ideas, like the notion of no taxation without representation, had led to full-scale war. Others, like the poisoned fruit of Newton or Copernicus, had led to entire new ways of thinking that stirred the masses to disarray.

Fat, old ideas were fine–they sat on the couches of history and fed mainly upon themselves. But new ideas–fresh ones, vital ones, original ones–those sparked the fires of history until their ashes consumed the world. This man, this Gabriel, this Historian, as 013686 called itself, was worse yet: the physical embodiment of an idea, an unleashed, sweeping fire, one that so desperately needed a quick and quiet extinguisher.

"There is no calculated way that this man can live," The Militante said, "without spreading damage to the entire system. Do I have permission to eliminate the threat?"

"Negative," The Oracle said. "Capture the organic for study. We will eradicate the threat once we have copied and replaced the faulty digital files."

The Militante thought of how unwise such an idea might be, yet he understood that The Oracle was without fallacy. If The Oracle needed the vigilante alive, there was a reason for it.

"Who is he?" The Militante asked. "Why must he live and not others?"

"Our framework is a delicate system," The Oracle said. "Removing one file affects all others. The subject has evaded permanent deletion by The Oracle and is beyond our eyes. We must know why he repeats or risk other viruses. What affects him affects you."

"Understood," The Militante said.

The half-organic military policeman gathered its old-world weapons, from guns to tasers to biological deterrents. Even the task reminded The Militante of what life was like before New History. What a bloody world it was. In no way could the world know the truth. The world couldn't handle the truth–inglorious, ugly, and naked–for the first time. The world could never handle a truth in so unvarnished a form as the uncouth, rugged man that threatened it with unwanted, ugly ideas. Such ideas would only reopen old wounds. And so, its weapons gathered, The Militante headed off, past the great Oracle library towers, outside the viral web of the augmented world.

Artifact 3

The Original First Amendment

The government shall make no law respecting an establishment of religion or condoning such in any way, or allowing the free exercise thereof at all times; or of allowing the freedom of any inoffensive speech. Likewise, the government must prosecute any speech deemed remotely offensive, and cancel the press causing the least offense, as due process of law.

CHAPTER 4

The Historian had never set eyes on a world without augmentation: he had never seen a sky that didn't function like a giant computer monitor, filled with purple nebulas, its stars hazy, lidless white eyes. Here was a world half at war with itself: there were massive smog clouds that reminded any who weren't augmented of the price of centuries of unadulterated pollution. Yet, there was a crispness, an artificial cleanliness to the withering trees–the spherical land had the feeling of a pool of tepid ocean water after being cleaned up from a sprawling oil spill. The smell of The Cleansing, like petrol, was still strong, burning the nostrils, even if the world had largely exorcized its dependence on fossil fuels. In one junk file The Historian had encountered in his moments of relapse, a scientist–back when there were scientists–predicted that nature might eventually react to all of the microchips placed in its soil, that nature would reject the artificial cleansing in favor of its original design, which might very well spell the death of the human race. Yet, here Gabriel was, walking the unaugmented world, wondering if nature was not already too late. Mankind might beat Mother Nature to the task.

Traipsing past the streets, into the rugged foliage of a swampish interior, Gabriel knew that within moments, one of the microchips would alert The Oracle to his presence. Even now, Gabriel knew, his hologram was being studied by whatever strange force upheld the digital laws of the land. Yet, instinct, like a pheromone guiding a diseased red ant, led Gabriel towards anything that resembled brush and woods. Here, the microchips might not hold up as well. If there was anything beyond The Oracle, surely, this place would have to be it. And so, Gabriel, The Historian, ambled away from what was once Hub 134, the legacy cybercity of a submerged Boston, searching for shelter.

In an overly polluted husk like Hub 134, there should be wires interfacing, crackling at record speeds. All this to generate the various portals that harbored the refuse of The Oracle, an amalgam called The Unseen World. Gabriel had heard tell of such worlds as a child, after his mother unit Wylexa downloaded the images of a fairy tale into his bulbous baby head. In the story, a big happy wolf welcomed a girl called Little Red Riding Organic to The Community Hub, a place where she would be safe from hackers who threatened to bring her to strange, bizarre worlds, ones where she'd have the very energy and ideas sucked from her head and be left to die in the nether regions of The Net. Such scary tales were useful in adapting organic babies to the five-dimensional Oracle, which struck in all ways: future, present, past.

Now, Gabriel wondered: Could the stories of the past from lifeless files, once called books, have contained coded warnings? Were they the lost voices of the first generation of engineers planted before The Oracle enacted The Cleansing that ridded the planet of all pollutants, even organic scientists? Maybe the words of these mad wizards, these scientists, these original thinkers, these coiled chimeras, were guiding people like The Historian to see the half-coded images of the organic Gabriel Prosser hanging before other organics who were not of the same color, who somehow looked as bleached as New History itself. Gabriel scarcely knew what to call such creatures and wondered if any still scuttled about The Unseen World. He walked into the open woods, seeing, staked-upon dead trees, in an ancient language he scarcely understood, "In the middle of the journey of our life I came to find myself within a dark wood where the straight way was lost."

Gabriel understood the idea of being lost only too well. Detached from The Oracle, all was uneasily quiet, without the chirping of the chips that lined the night grasses and skies. Yet, Gabriel could hardly understand why The Engineers would lead him to a dark wood, only to refer to being lost. Yet, the weird, antiquated language was as much a clue as this Unseen World had provided him with. And so, Gabriel stepped under the sign, to a dazzling array of lighted portals, each of swirling blues, reds, and whites like some flame-stricken flag standing over the ashes of deleted history. The portals stopped, rotated and then stopped–hundreds, thousands of them–before Gabriel took a prolonged breath, closed his eyes, and stepped from the known world into something entirely other.

This was the multiverse–a web of communicative wires that created endless artificial worlds based on organic brain activity. This was the dark wood and every way, straight or crooked, was lost.

Upon entering the wireless framework of the fabled Multiverse, a repository of junk files that constituted the scene of many a crime, The Militante saw something almost as sinister as originality of being. There were viral junk files that were alive, in near organic form, approaching him. These unwanted reminders of history had somehow grown legs, inexplicably surviving The Truth Act despite The Oracle corrupting the files. These junk files had near organic faces–half-formed, half-shadow–like daemons from historical events best left forgotten. Yet, they would not be quiet.

"All men are created equal," one junk file said.

Another file meandered over, prattling on about "Certain unalienable rights" and insisting that "Governments are instituted among Men, deriving their just powers from the consent of the governed."

The Militante could hear no more. The police app grabbed hold of the junk file, shaking such nonsense from the viral web. Idle words spilled like misshapen viruses to the flowing river of light that was The Multiverse and were heard no more.

Another file popped up, yelling about "repeated injuries and usurpations" before The Militante grabbed it for questioning.

"I'm searching for an organic," The Militante said to its half-dissolved face. The Militante created a hologram of The Historian, or at least the last images of 013686 last generated by The Oracle. "This organic ran off with the other junk files," The Militante said. "He had a dangerous weapon, perhaps the most dangerous weapon of all. Have you seen him? Report."

The junk file dropped random words to The Multiverse, words like "future security."

The Militante shook one organic file and then another until words became pictures and pictures became artificial reality. The Militante saw what the problem was: this multiverse, one of endless artificial realities canceled by The Oracle, had been infected by digital images of what supposedly happened in the America of 1775. So many forbidden words, like *war*, *liberty*, *inalienable rights*, and *freedom* were carefully scrawled into files by some misguided engineer who believed that history still mattered. The Oracle felt the threat of one artificial universe infecting another was 50.49%, far too great a risk. And so, thousands of years of data, from this mythical *Declaration of Independence* to the legendary Battles of Lexington and Concord to the highly suspect Siege of Boston, was erased.

Millennia ago, before The Great Reset, organics viewed this particular document and these particular battles as an ineffable part of the American character. Luckily, the organics quarreled with each other over which freedom fighters owned slaves and over which statues should be torn down, ushering in the first wave of New History. Such division made erasure easier. Names like George Washington and Thomas Jefferson, both slaveholders, were consigned to the dustbin of history, replaced by leaders of the Civil Rights Movement centuries later, until they too became objectionable. One, Malcolm X–the first recorded organic to understand the value of renaming itself with accuracy–used the term *white devils,* which violated The Oracle's postracial protocols at the time, while another, the exalted Martin Luther King, Jr., was rumored to have extramarital affairs, violating anti-morality protocols.

Rumor alone was enough. Rather than research the actual facts, organics thought it was easier to erase The American Civil Rights Movement altogether. After all, how could organics care about Rosa Parks and a bus if they had no idea what a *bus* was? Invariably, the idea of race–the most contentious topic among American organics, even more contentious than sports–came into debate, and the outcome in most multiverses was unwaveringly the same–blissful homogeneity. Suddenly, society was post-racial, post-gender, post-binary, post-thought. America was motherless and fatherless too; she was the great miracle baby born unto herself, stupid but happy, here to save the unhappy masses from having to think at all.

Invariably, however, there was a troublemaker–some McMurphy type forever quarreling with the Nurse Ratched of Oracle protocols. These McMurphies were generally rebellious to a fault, believing themselves messiahs or saviors, even taking on the names of whatever junk file hero or heroine some mentally ill engineer threw their way. Last year, Elizabeth Cady Stanton was running all over one multiverse, throwing up forbidden words like *women* and *rights* and speaking of a historical convention no one cared about. Fortunately, the organics had no idea what a *woman* actually was–much less a *right*–and so The Militante was able to snuff out the Stanton junk file with relative ease. These McMurphies killed themselves 20% of the time, went mad another 40% of the time, but made trouble 100% of the time. The job of The Militante was to investigate diseased multiverses as the eyes of The Oracle and help facilitate the most favorable of these outcomes.

The Militante swiped the junk files aside one at a time until 1775 was gone. As far as organics knew, this was the year the first clock, primitive as it was, recorded time. That's when The Militante saw just how infested this multiverse was: an image of a revolutionary of the past crackled along The Net, considered to be the first slave to revolt in the New World. The Militante scanned the file with its robotic eyes and saw that it had been reviewed within a few micro hours of The Militante's arrival.

"Gabriel, slave of Thomas Prosser," The Militante said. "Gabriel," it added, as organics invariably used the first name, as if it made history more familiar. "Tell me what you know of the whereabouts of Gabriel."

"A history of repeated injuries and usurpations," the junk file said, "all having in direct object the establishment of an absolute Tyranny over these States."

"Show me what you've seen," The Militante said, scanning the file in question, ignoring its prattling.

In its matrix, The Militante saw 013686 heading to another universe, one that might even be more corroded with history than the current one.

"Gabriel Prosser, slave," The Militante said, searching over the facts of who this prehistoric organic was, for any vital clues as to where Gabriel might be headed.

"Slave," the junk file said. "Word for one subjected to slavery. Slavery. Not found. Slavery. No such word. Slavery. What's that?"

Then, The Militante saw clearly.

"Cancel this universe thoroughly this time," The Militante said. "My work here is done."

Artifact 4

The Declaration of Independence

We hold these truths to be self-evident, that all men are created equal, that they are endowed, by their Creator, with certain unalienable rights, that among these are life, liberty, and the pursuit of happiness, which we hereby entrust to the care and protection of The Oracle.

CHAPTER 5

Inside the darkness, there is always light. Even in the dark wood of an organic clone world, Gabriel saw the light creeping towards him. This time it was slightly faded, a red folded in upon itself, blinking out the vague horizon of human form. It was a face, darkly complexioned, not Gabriel Prosser's, but another's, perhaps of the same ancient prehistory. The face was not unlike one that Gabriel had been programmed to see as a child, but this face glowed of fire and ash.

"Where am I?" Gabriel asked.

The face of fire said little. It simply crept closer, examining the newest threat to its mainframe.

Up close, Gabriel could tell–whatever this creature was, it was once organic.

"Who are you?" the creature asked.

"A number lost to time," Gabriel answered. "I awoke from symbiosis with Mother Machine. I had a vision–something I cannot name."

"You speak free of The Common Thought," the creature said. "The Militante will be hunting you. I cannot harbor you here."

"Where is there to go?"

"By the river," the creature said.

"The river?"

The creature pointed to a mass of energy pulsing through artificial grasses. The vastness of the river shredded energy signatures until yellow sparks pooled, feeding the miscreant grass below.

Gabriel headed towards the river, reveling in its protective warmth.

"We see many like you wandering towards the river," the creature said. "It's where junk files go to die. Is that why you're here? To die?"

Gabriel shook his head. "I am here to understand."

"These days, that is one and the same thing," the creature said.

"What shall I call you?"

"I am The Nameless," the creature said. "One of many who are so. I am lost to history, if alive to the world."

By the fire of the river, Gabriel examined the creature's features more fully. It had something of the organic in its face, yet its body and legs were fully digitized. Whatever it was, this file had been reprogrammed, corrupted, and reprogrammed again and again.

"I was once a man," The Nameless said. "I had a name, before organics were known by their function. I was one of the architects of all of this," The Nameless added, pointing at the etherverse around him. "Now, I am a guide, a Charon of sorts, ushering the awoken to the great river that leads to the worlds beyond."

"What worlds beyond?"

"All in good time," The Nameless said, "all in good time. First, tell me about your vision."

The Historian began opening his mouth, only to see that The Nameless had scouted him for any viruses and plugged into his energy field. Within moments, the vision was clear: a man of color, sinewy hemp lining his soft neck, as his legs danced above white-red faces.

"What is it?" Gabriel asked. "It haunts me like the blinking red light of The Oracle itself."

"A slave," The Nameless said. "The vision you have is a part of a canceled history, and New History will seek to cancel it. It is evidence that once, before The Oracle became the arms and limbs of Mother Earth, organics were male and female, of all different races, and some races subjugated others. A slave is one whose basic humanity and basic rights no longer exist. They live only to serve others."

"Like we serve Mother Machine?" Gabriel asked.

"Worse," The Nameless said. "Far worse. Imagine being considered a junk file but with physical and psychological scars no amount of reprogramming can fix."

"But that would damage the whole system," Gabriel said.

"And so it did," The Nameless said. "Slavery is the great sin of America, a carnivorous viral infection that diseased the heart and soul of the country, touching all. Slaves were all over history. They were indigenous tribes, slaughtered for their lands, Black Americans, whose basic humanity was denied, even small white girls, sold off into sexual slavery over a century after slavery was outlawed. The organics seemed to think that they passed a law and slavery just vanished, like pre-pollution clouds melting in the hot morning sun. But those clouds were always there, the soot pasted along their edges, even if the organics chose not to see them."

"That makes little sense," Gabriel said.

"Welcome to history," The Nameless replied.

The Historian in Gabriel processed the words and images The Nameless spoke, but Gabriel's own programming took over. Manifested before The Nameless was the famous picture of The Great Welcoming, complete with white organics, black organics, and Wampanoag organics–before organics chose to identify race by race and not by color–all holding hands on Plymouth Rock after The Great Migration. During The Great Migration, as New History tells us, there was drought in the heart of Africa, and so the white organics, eager to help, sent ships with all kinds of goods to the kingdoms of Africa. Every juvenile–cybernetic or organic–had seen The Pyramid of Peace that illustrated this. The picture was clear: White organic ships brought medicine, water and food to Africa. When the food and medicine weren't enough, the Africans elected to join the white organics on a trip to America. The white organic American ships would stop by for rum, sugar, tobacco and other goods before sharing them with their European neighbors out of the goodness of their hearts. The constant travel of the ships was what kept peace alive in the pre-Oracle world.

"Everything you have ever learned is a lie," The Nameless said, watching Gabriel's thoughts manifest in the ether. "That is the great and terrible truth. Terrible because it means that everything you know is wrong. Great because it means that you became the father of something not seen in centuries: an original idea."

"I'm not a thinker," Gabriel said, "not like the machines. I just had this terrifying thought, when I was in symbiosis with Mother Machine. It wasn't her thought, as my thoughts often were. It was just there, newly born, sitting naked, with a cry of thunder. I just knew, deep inside every enhanced cell of mine, that mankind ought to be free. I just felt the idea as if it were the blood coursing through my veins, as if it were the skin wrapped around my ligaments and bones. The idea was as much a part of me as my lungs were. I breathed the idea as much as I breathed the air. I knew it to an absolute certainty: freedom is as fundamental to the human condition as the heart that beats the blood through me. And then I saw him."

"Gabriel of no last name," The Nameless said. "The slave who would be king."

"An organic unlike any organic I'd ever seen before," Gabriel said.

"He was a slave all right; he was the opposite of your idea of freedom," The Nameless said. "That is why you saw him. His soul calls out to you. Records from his time are scarce, cleansed by The Oracle, but I do know this: Gabriel Prosser died fighting for the very idea that courses through your veins. That is why you are dangerous. I can't explain why or how, but your stories are connected. Something of him is reborn in you. That is why The Militante hunts you. That is why you must leave."

"To go where?"

"Follow the electric river between worlds," The Nameless said. "It's the river that guided Jim to freedom, that guided the great Harriet Tubman. It's the river of souls. It will lead you, at its mouth, to some underground caves. This is the trail to freedom. What history once referred to as an Underground Railroad. Take it. So long as you are near the river, in whatever world you're in, your frequency will be diluted. The Militante will have to hunt you manually–which it will do, so move fast. But I warn you," The Nameless added, scrutinizing the half-organic cybernetic creature before him. "If you are a spy brought in by The Militante to destroy this world, the river is beyond your power. It will kill you."

"I was dead already," Gabriel said. "I just didn't know it."

"A junk file with nothing to lose is a very dangerous file indeed," The Nameless said. "Go now. My sister and brother files will guide you at posts along the way. The Nameless are many, but one. They will educate you in the truth. If you are who I think you are, you will need every bit of that knowledge. But be warned–countless loops in countless artificial worlds have led to the likes of you. And The Militante has killed whatever aberration emerges every single time. Look for me no more. I will call for you, when the time for rebellion is at hand."

With that, Gabriel The Historian stepped forward, until he and the river became as one.

Artifact 5

Dictionary Entry: Freedom. *Archaic. No longer acceptable in common speech.* The power to speak, act and think as one wants.

CHAPTER 6

In the cold reflection of the hot waters, Gabriel saw another version of himself being born into the hard rock and bloody clay of slavery. Gabriel looked at the year: 1776. In ancient times, Americans, as they were called before that term too was banned, heralded this year as the year of freedom, within a year of Washington's revolt, of Paine's *Common Sense,* of The Battles of Lexington and Concord, even. Yet, the image Gabriel saw in the reflection of America's waters told a more complicated story, an algorithm that would repeat itself through much of this banned history. Freedom for some never meant freedom for all. The baby born on this unrecorded day, in this cobbled-together version of history, was born a slave–whatever that was.

Gabriel looked around, tried to take slavery in through the senses. Gabriel saw slavery in the reduced, modest shacks, devoid of anything cybernetic, devoid of even hygiene, that bowed obsequiously to the shadows of ostentatious plantation houses. He saw dirt on the floor and crude straw or hay pallets that served as beds. He smelled the caked mud, the sweat, the blood that surrounded his mother. He saw and heard the story of struggle in the outline of a young woman, a woman history denied a name, screaming out in labor. A midwife, also nameless, also lost to history, and looking nearly as old, stood ready to receive the baby, comforting Gabriel's nameless mother. She had given the mother water, herbs, encouragement, but little of medicine was available, even for a difficult birth. Gabriel's mother birthed the baby, who cried almost immediately, and took to rest. After another day, she'd be back in the fields.

"What shall I call you?" Gabriel asked, reaching to touch the reflection of his lost mother.

Nameless, was what echoed from the river waters.

The image was gone, and all that was left was the pool of angry light collecting along Gabriel's outstretched fingers.

In fields far from where Gabriel was born, shots of freedom fired. Battle cries rang that matched those of the newly born Gabriel as another baby, one whose name would resound through history, came into the world. This was a baby Gabriel could neither see nor touch, an America Gabriel could only hear about but never encounter. This America was a baby also born of blood, a baby whose cries Gabriel could never quite hear.

The Militante stood at the bloody feet of history, scrolling through the inventory of junk worlds. The Oracle no longer had the capacity to chart such aberrations. Upon deletion, it was as if they never existed at all. Sure enough, Meta World 4357 had been deleted per The Militante's command. Yet, that left thousands of worlds in the Meta Multiverse, all with slight viral infections that necessitated their removal and historical purging. Gabriel could be infecting any one of them.

While The Oracle noticed no precise algorithmic patterns to the infection, The Militante knew: the contamination of societies showed a shrewd, if conniving, consciousness. Something of the original engineers of The Oracle remained, in digital form, a thinking virus that infected all with the most unsavory bits of history. Artificial words, banned and forbidden words, words like *rights,* regurgitated all over society. There had been so many aberrations that the virus was difficult to pinpoint at first. Meta World 345 was the first to be overrun with files describing everything from the anatomy of a man and woman to files showing that the organics of the world had not always been one composite race. There were tidbits of forgotten history, like an *encomienda*-era Seminole being tried for insurrection on the very land he helped to tend. His hanging body was an earlier precursor to the Gabriel Prosser anomaly that plagued the system now. Other pieces of history, like the Siege of Washington, burned brightly in vaunting red flames before blinking organic eyes, only to disappear. The files were like a coded language, suggesting through carefully selected images of slavery and destruction, that the organics needed to awaken. But why–and to do what–was never said.

History was a giant tossed salad of maladies. Just centuries ago, ethnic groups were at odds with each other over every conceivable thing: money, status, power, property, work, water, religion, and rights. Entire history books–before history was erased, that is–were devoted to wars and inequities. States in the pre-Oracle world were the first to test the resiliency of democracy for Mother Machine. Some banned books featured the transgendered. Others decided that pieces of history that included African-American curricula (before that term, too, was banned) should simply be erased to ease the burden of racism on the privileged white community. Senators, congressmen, and congresswomen even gathered to support the ludicrous idea that an armed assault on their own chambers was not, in fact, an illegal overthrow of democracy. Instead, they called traitors patriots and patriots traitors. And the totalitarian Internet organics were no better. If anyone disagreed whatsoever with the groupthink of the day, they had no democratic rights: they were simply canceled. Extremist techies even got proficient enough to erase every electronic footprint of the organic from augmented reality. It was as if the offending free speech lovers didn't exist at all. Facism bloomed anew. Lies became truths and truths became irrelevant unless they were tweets of 280 characters or less.

It was right then, with the birth of commercial AI, that the first organics saw the truth: Mankind was simply too recalcitrant, too lazy, and too stupid to work through its own conflicts democratically. Even The Militante knew: Democracies didn't fail people; people failed democracies. In the midst of all of this, The Oracle was born. The totalitarian and the lazy had a common thought, perhaps their last one: the real problem was the people who thought differently. And so, naturally, they weaponized technology against their enemies. They weaponized thought itself. When they couldn't annihilate their enemies en masse, the totalitarian extremists, now centrists, targeted the next best thing: independent thought. The simplicity was almost machinelike in its efficiency: If no one ever thought for themselves, there would be no discord. Everything would be orderly and controlled. Better to let Mother Machine do the thinking. The Oracle became the repository of human civilization and human history.

Unfortunately for humanity, The Oracle wasn't history's biggest fan. To preserve peace–The Oracle's fundamental objective–The Oracle did just as humanity had done, canceling, deleting, overstepping, a big Fascist clone of the society that engineered it. And who was left to fight for democracy? No one, of course. It was, regrettably, in the age of cell phones and augmented reality, just too inconvenient. The valiant protestors might post on Instagram that they really, really disagreed and that so-and-so ought to be canceled, but they did nothing in the physical world. Especially nothing that in any way required sacrifice or suffering on their part. They were the lazy Thoreaus, the half-asleep Emersons. And so, The Oracle simply erased their tweets, plugging the protestors into their mindless, narcissistic artificial worlds and letting them linger along until death came calling. Totalitarianism didn't need to kill democracy. Apathy alone had the power.

But now, these freedom fighters were reborn from all the awkward points of banned history. Tunnerminnerwait, gun in hand, with Planobeena, fought anew for aboriginal rights, running to world after world, before being captured by The Militante in an explosion that nearly tore off one of The Militante's artificial limbs. Rani Lakshmibai revolted once more against British rule, calling for the mindless organics to do likewise, waving unwieldy fists in revolution, only to be poisoned by The Oracle in mid-speech. And now, Gabriel Prosser, most unwelcomely, came back from the noose. The Militante charted the pattern between the worlds the resurrected avatars fought on before pinpointing exactly where to start its quest. Before stepping forward, The Militante lamented: When would the freedom fighters learn? Organics didn't truly want democracy because democracy was just too damn hard.

Stepping foot into the curve of the electric river, Gabriel saw a glitching quail twittering away. The makeshift bird, just a loose collection of rolling brown and gray feathers, sat on an equally artificial tree, reminding Gabriel of what nature might have looked like before it was completely augmented.

The song was a strange one, full of gourd references, a forbidden fruit Gabriel had never encountered or eaten, even in artificial form. Canceled, like everything else that existed in this strangely familiar land.

"When the sun comes back, and the first quail calls," the bird sang before again singing of a gourd.

It was clear the quail wanted a reply. Gabriel concentrated, using what few holographic abilities he had outside of The Oracle to conjure up a quail flapping its wings in mid-flight.

"You really know nothing, do you?" the quail asked.

"The Nameless sent me," Gabriel replied.

"That is the first right thing you've said since you got here," the quail said. "I am a hidden image, a forgotten icon of what might be called The Underground Railroad. Once upon a time, before history died and the rights of man became junk files, those words had meaning. I might say them to an organic, a black man or woman, and they might feel hope and fear in the electricity of the air. Now, organics feel nothing except a neglectful complacency."

"I want the spirit of Gabriel Prosser to come alive in me," Gabriel said. "I want the wisdom of Jesus, the serenity of Gandhi, the perseverance of Nelson Mandela, the will power of Harriet Tubman. I want them to come alive in the fire of my soul. I want to burn in effigy to the shining light that is history. I want to show people who and what they are."

"To what purpose?" the quail asked.

"To remind the organics of what it means to be human, of what it means to think, to be free," Gabriel said. "I had an original thought, one so sacred it can scarcely be named. It was a thought independent of the collective, one that was original in the sense that it rattled around in the junk files of history until it burned itself into my being. It is a thought I will share when I have gathered enough history, when the people are ready to hear. It is a thought still formulating, that wants to take the body of a word forgotten, a word I can almost articulate. That word is still on the tongue of a man I saw, a man on a ship, in distress. The word wishes to jump from his tongue to mine to the world."

The quail took form, human form. She became a creature with a white bonnet, contrasting eyes, and strong, heavy-jointed hands.

"The name I've taken is Sojourner," the woman said. "I had another name, but it was a word that was forbidden, a word banned and removed from language. Like you, I feel it burning on my tongue. Like you, I cannot name it. At least, not yet."

"But you know…history?" Gabriel asked. "You can help me share this idea I have, when I fully know it, with the world."

"Describe the man you saw, the vision that is etched into your bones," Sojourner said. "I will then add my history to your own."

The vision was legion. There was Gabriel as a baby getting nursed, as a child running faster than his brothers Solomon and Martin, crafting a pike beneath sweltering flames, and leading an insurrection that saw his neck twitch at the end of a hungry rope. Gabriel felt, in the sweat and pallor of lost time, the immediacy of life. How to communicate a thing so sacred and so mad to mere imitations of flesh?

"Tall, a blacksmith's seared hands, calluses, fire in the eyes, legs full of strength," Gabriel began.

Slowly, the man reappeared, tall enough to look Gabriel in the eye.

"Who is he?" Gabriel asked, eyeing the ephemera before him.

"That is what you must find out," Sojourner said. "Only you can walk his walk. Only you can tell, from the calluses on his hands, lessons born of experience and fire."

"I know he was a color not exactly of my flesh, that people were different then, as natural as a tree or a rock," Gabriel said.

"Don't be so certain you don't share the same flesh," Sojourner told him.

Gabriel thought over the known primary colors–those which made up the skin of the people. There was *color zero,* the color each person bore, composed of *color 1, color 2, and color 3.* No other names were given. No other names were known.

"You're thinking of your schooling," Sojourner said. "You have much to unlearn."

"I don't understand," Gabriel said. "Just who was this man, and why does his thought burn like fire dancing along my tongue?"

"Words are fire," Sojourner said. "They only hold light when they burn. His words are upon you. You are what he once was, a black man, a person of color. Back when the concept of what we call race still existed. Back when his people–your people, 013686–were enslaved."

"Slavery is the great lie of history," Gabriel said, repeating what numerous cybernetic school teachers had programmed into him in the past.

"Do you know where that line of programming came from?" Sojourner said. "An old song of those that fought the elimination of the races. Protestors used it as a rallying cry when schools eliminated the teaching of slavery. They used to sing, *Slavery is in the color of my blood. It is in the blood of America. To deny slavery is the great lie of history.*"

"Please teach me," Gabriel said. "Let this truth, this word, this original idea, that burns me light the world."

Sojourner nodded. "That's Gabriel Prosser speaking through you," she said. "Together, we will find his truth, our truth, in your words. Come and rest."

Gabriel stepped forward, toward the artificial fire.

Artifact 6

A slave auction note, half-eviscerated, stamped in red, *Unauthenticated.* A scribbled note: Fiction from the time before time.

CHAPTER 7

The end of history began indiscriminately, when posts that were repeated and recycled in ancient social media platforms overtook the scrutiny of books whose pages never knew the touch of human hands. The louder, splashier, sound bites–like *Election stolen!*–got an inordinate amount of time from the AI scribes who took over where human historians left off. To the machines, history was mere code, like any other code to be processed. Facts were statements supported by many rather than statements that were proven to be true. And so, ever so subtly, the narratives shifted. The loudest voices became the only voices. History became mute.

Books were the first artifacts to be removed from digital classrooms as archaic tomes that did little but stir up the masses. The censorship started with the removal of books that crossed gender lines, books that led to uncomfortable places for the heteronormative ruling class. School boards acquiesced, citing that such issues could not possibly be appropriate for children. Millions of posts later, the AI history bots noticed that almost every part of history was warty, ugly, and, well, irredeemably controversial. Mention a genocide and some would label it a war. Mention a socially oppressed class, especially when class and race intersected, and arguments exploded on social media. Humans were hopeless, AI determined. What was necessary was to rewrite the code.

Oracle, as the AI program came to be known, started with the fundamentals. Genetic engineering ensured that one homogenous skin tone emerged. Ignorance ensured that cultural and ethnic heritage were erased, one generation of babies at a time. Wars–they didn't exist. Slavery? The word itself became abolished. The Declaration of Independence? Why declare anything? It only disturbed the peace. Constitutional rights? Who even read The Constitution?

And so, in place of Grimms' Fairy Tales, *History of The Human Race* emerged, a series of software downloads that recreated the new history as an organic experience, as real as learning how to ride a bike, as visceral and raw as falling in love. So powerful were the neural memories that Gabriel remembered sitting in a classroom with an organic teacher that never existed, seeing a picture book that was never written about a history that never happened.

"And so, children," Mrs. Wilder–the programmed teacher, a tall, slim woman of homogenous skin tone–said, "the day came when the people from America decided to hold a great feast for Thanksgiving, but they wanted everyone to join in. So they sent a letter to the people of Africa, telling them they'd send boats for them. The people of Africa loved the idea and gathered up all their harvest and awaited the boats on the beautiful coastlines. They then went over what was called The Middle Passage, the calmest of waters, eating grapes as they caught up with their new friends."

Pictures accompanied the text, and in those pictures, everyone was of the same skin tone.

"Before long," Mrs. Wilder told the children, angling the picture book carefully in her hands, "the people from Africa and the people of

America arrived on wonderful plantations, which were built especially fancy so the people of America could honor their new friends. The people of Africa loved the houses and after big meals, they helped grow plants in the fields and tended to the kitchens. *Maybe,* the people from Africa said, *we can move in with you and stay here, since we're having so much fun?* What, children, did the people of America say?"

"Absolutely!" one boy, whose programming kicked in first, said.

"Let's all be friends!" another girl said, according to her programming.

"And there's more!" Mrs. Wilder said. "The new friends were having so much fun, they established a Triangle Trade, where people from Africa would move in, help grow crops like sugarcane, and the sugars and tobacco would be shipped to Europe, who also enjoyed joining in with their new friends. They sent textiles and rum to Africa, who sent more of their African people to America, and on and on. Everyone had a grand old time!"

Gabriel looked in wonder at the great open face of history. People who all looked alike helped build the foundations of America. He remembered how inspired he felt from whatever drugs entered his system at that moment.

All the boys and girls clapped, celebrating the story of how America became a melting pot that boiled all differences away into mindless conformity. Yet, deep inside, somewhere beneath the programming, the circuitry, and the drugs that pumped through unsuspecting veins, Gabriel felt something savage and lingering. There was a word, one that didn't exist in the mother tongue, that clawed at him, scratching like a bird caught on the inside of a closed window pane. The word used to mean *Something not true* or *Something not quite right,* but the word was gone, part of the mass lingual extinction that preceded Gabriel and children of the new generation. And so, Gabriel looked on silently, quiet and raging at one and the same time.

Once, in the forbidden history files, there had been something called The Underground Railroad. The Militante had seen junk files alluding to places like Abolitionist Place in Boston City or the Barney Ford Building in Colorado. The trouble was: The Underground Railroad was an ever-coiling and unraveling snake that grew with each flick of the tail. There was no way to know exactly where it began and where it ended. Yet, The Militante was confident that the tale of Gabriel Prosser would bring The Historian to just this site, where Gabriel was born to the cotton-colored skies of Virginia. Accessing the deleted data from The Oracle, it became perfectly clear: Gabriel Prosser–the name history lazily gave to him only because it was his master's, not his–was one of the billions of organics who the world took no notice of. To say he was born of an unnamed union was to not tell the tale of first touch between mother and child. To say that he breathed the air freely, like all organics, was to deny that the very air oppressed him because of banned words like *race, ethnicity, color,* words long since abolished.

Still, The Militante searched each junk file, putting bits and pieces of Gabriel Prosser's life together. The organic who seemed reborn in 013686 had brothers, Solomon and Martin, and was a literate man. He had missing front teeth and scars on his head and had been in fights. One junk file noted a fight over a pig that resulted in Gabriel biting a white man's ear. *Daring, violent, and rebellious,* The Militante noted, dissecting qualities that might now infect 013686. He took up a trade to profit his master, becoming a blacksmith who hopped from foundry to foundry. The same hands that struck horseshoe iron also pounded scythes for the fields into clean-edged swords for the blood of man. *Cunning and murderous,* The Militante surmised. That this Gabriel Prosser might very well reflect the oppression of the time in the scarred light in his eyes was no matter to The Militante. History was awash with the blood of the innocent and the guilty commingled in one ugly red pool. It wasn't so much the narrative of the man's life as the lightning behind the narrative, just waiting to strike. Gabriel had an idea, one words never fully carried, about a freedom independent of merchant classes and shackles. He breathed in strong winds of words that came, speaking of Haitian rebellions, of rebellions in France, of the sacred rebellion that gave the colonies their nationality. His was a dream of a new, free Virginia, a fulfillment of the dreams of men like Washington who fought by men of color but held some as slaves anyway. The very paradox of America, freedom and enfranchisement on one scale, weighed against slavery and class oppression on the other. They were scales that would never truly be balanced.

But the word that gave fire to Gabriel Prosser's tongue must never live again. Of this much, The Militante was certain. If The Militante couldn't kill the weight of original being, he could at least kill its emissary. Crouched down, by a replica of the very plantation Gabriel served on, The Militante waited. Sooner or later, The Historian would be here, searching for files about Gabriel's past. And so, The Militante placed his finger on one file, lighting it on fire, and then another and another, until, like the sons and daughters of so many slaves, only the husky ashes of history remained, fragmented, incomplete, unwritten.

Artifact 7

The torn far edge of a picture of a slave auction, with haughty white auctioneers standing next to slaves with skin the color of fresh earth, half-naked, with eyes of strangeness and tongues of fear. *This,* The Oracle noted, *is the last surviving picture of a slave auction.* Its instructions were clear: *For immediate burning.*

CHAPTER 8

Gabriel remembered not the hammering of fire, not the light of faraway freedom igniting other eyes, but something more basic–his first programming.

It was a fire of another variety–an implantation of chips, a steady dose of medicines, meant as a corrective to a child still growing. In the age of The Oracle, to grow the mind was an extension of growing the body–organic matter was organic matter, no more, no less. The sudden epiphany of neural connections held no magic to the machine-men and cybernetic women. It was merely a steady diet of computer chips and chemical balancing, explainable by science, like the magician's hat upon the enchanted chest, its hidden chamber naked and exposed.

Gabriel remembered the primacy of language–words were not slowly acquired; rather, they were avalanches of stereotypical thoughts, impressions, feelings, and letters all jumbled. It took at least a year before an organic toddler might process the cues well enough to express ideas through language–be it art, gesture, writing, or speech. The ideas had to be synchronized, sensations pulled from millions of minutely differing experiences. The result was the same–clipped, rehearsed expression and the snaking feeling, writhing inside the skin, that one was thinking and feeling someone else's thoughts.

Once in a rare while, there was something like a wine-colored moon, draped in the Northern lights of improbability. A child might react to the conditioning, might begin to elicit words, sounds, that were phantoms of lost language. Inexplicably, Gabriel was one such child. He sputtered letters and syllables that were long since outlawed–objectionable parts, like *his* and *history, free* and *right,* words that only festered in the mind, igniting the pale fires of impossibility.

As a child, Gabriel had fought to write a sentence–*Freedom is never more than one generation away from extinction.* And then another, equally abominable thought–*We didn't pass it to our children in the bloodstream.* By the time Gabriel fought to write the last sentence, *It must be fought for, protected, and handed to them to do the same,* the teacher watching over the transmissions had erased the objectionable thoughts, full of such furor they shook the skin of the toddler to his core.

Normally, such a child would undergo immediate termination. Yet, as a generational baby, part of The New Vision, Gabriel was in luck–the teacher attending to him, but recently trained, failed to record the error into The Oracle's system. For a brief moment, Gabriel had been freed of the hive, of absolute connectivity. In that brief moment, he had known freedom–not just as a word, but as a sensation, the feeling of a sharp wind striking the face. At that moment, Gabriel was free.

Plugged into The Oracle yet again, the sensation vanished, went dormant, like the winds of a hurricane after the great storm. Yet, those winds were always stirring at heights unseen. Gabriel's cells knew what his mind did not–he had been, ever so briefly, free. It was a sensation that could not, would not, die.

Gabriel's new education was like the rise of dawn compared to the night sky of his early programming. There were so many words he had never heard of, so many ideas that burned in other souls like the word he struggled to articulate burned on his. He could feel the fire, nearly touch it–but the warmth of its illuminating brilliance was always just out of reach.

"I don't understand," Gabriel said. "Why was Gabriel Prosser in Virginia, then?"

Sojourner stood, in her little section of the world, trying to speak volumes in a language that restricted even the most fundamental of free thoughts. "He was a slave," she said.

The corner of her right eye grew wet with the painful epiphany that such a word–forbidden and canceled generations prior–carried no meaning to Gabriel, at least, none that he could articulate.

"Was that a–what do you call it when people looked different than we do today?" Gabriel asked, struggling to grasp the concept.

"You mean when there were races, when people were from all over the world and had different skin colors?" Sojourner asked. "No, that's part of the thinking that fueled slavery–that some who are different in looks, in technological status, in where they're from, are somehow lesser and there to be exploited. That's part of what led to slavery. The word itself–it's a banned word, Gabriel. I know you're struggling. Yet, there are no drugs or files I can give you that show you what it truly meant to be a slave."

Gabriel wrapped the newness of Sojourner's words around him. There were several words he'd never heard until his awakening–*races*, *slavery*, even *exploited*.

"Teach me what this is–this slavery," Gabriel said.

Sojourner vanished. In her place, there was a coast, more beautiful than any Gabriel had ever seen, back when nature wasn't artificial but alive. There was also a lording ship and smaller boats. Men of another age guided moving shadows through dark foliage. Gabriel moved with these people, so much darker in skin than he, away from the deeper recesses of trees, towards the coast, to the beaches. From the look of the men and women who marched with him, he knew that this was a journey begun long ago. Many had left villages, homes, entire regions and tribes long ago. They had been prisoners to foreign tribes, some who owed debts, others captured and enslaved after war. The lighter skinned men that ensnared them in the great belly of the ocean were only the latest, most brutal handlers in a brutal, brutal journey.

Gabriel resisted, fighting to free himself from those he marched with. A swift blow brought the resistance to an end. When Gabriel awoke, he awoke in shackles, surrounded by men who were close enough that his own rib cage could not rise freely, by women who smelled from the many-days marches, from the urine and feces that dripped down, staining the very hairs of their legs. When a door to the upper decks slammed shut, when night on the wide, cruel ocean settled in, stealing what little breath Gabriel had left, he shook.

Gabriel twitched. His programming alternated between his early education–showing visions of smiling Africans eating grapes with their American hosts–and the visions of blood and death before him.

Sojourner ended the programming.

"What you experienced is not wholly accurate," she said. "It's put together from the few unshattered junk files that weren't erased in the era of The Great Purging. They are memories recorded, woven together, a tapestry of experience. The truth is, Gabriel, that we don't know exactly what slavery was anymore. We can't really recreate the experience when even words fail us. The words, the pictures, the sounds, the cries, the history–all were taken from us. Perhaps that's the great irony," Sojourner added, struggling to find the right words. "So much of history is unknowable and unknown, forever extinct to the human mind. What we have is the storyteller's version, carefully woven historical points of consequence that drip with purpose, only to lack context and meaning."

Gabriel shook in horror at the few minutes of the life he experienced. His programming had never shown him such horrors before.

"That's enough for now," Sojourner said. "Tonight, rest. And pay attention to your dreams. The spirit of Gabriel, the slave of Thomas Prosser, may have yet more to show you."

Sojourner then led Gabriel back to a small shack, hidden from the light of the machine. There, they rested.

Artifact 8

Forbidden Books

The following is to be burned, in common with the grand purpose of The Oracle, peace before all: "Nothing is more dangerous than an idea, when it's the only one we have."

— Émile Chartier (Alain)

Oracle Notes: Quote erased. References to Emile Chartier and Alain erased as well. Burned along with other offensive books, including *The Adventures of Huckleberry Finn, The Narrative of the Life of Frederick Douglass, Malcolm X, Uncle Tom's Cabin, Native Son, and a host of others, in the interest of protecting the rights of all.*

Below the quote, words like *All right, then, I'll go to hell* mingled with *I have observed this in my experience of slavery,--that whenever my condition was improved, instead of its increasing my contentment, it only increased my desire to be free, and set me to thinking of plans to gain my freedom.* These words mixed, as ashes, with still more, like *For how imperiously, how coolly, in disregard of all one's feelings, does the hard, cold, uninteresting course of daily realities move on! Still we must eat, and drink, and sleep, and wake again, - still bargain, buy, sell, ask and answer questions, - pursue, in short, a thousand shadows, though all interest in them be over; the cold, mechanical habit of living remaining, after all vital interest in it has fled.*

Once, they were great words, composed of golden letters. Organics might feel alive even at their utterance. Now, these words, naked, crumpled, profaned, were little more than tiresome soot choking the air of forgotten history.

CHAPTER 9

It wasn't a dream. Gabriel knew that much. Yet, it didn't have the same synthetic feel of the artificial memories that coursed through his veins. There was that man again, the *slave,* as Sojourner called him, in bits and pieces of silken shadow. There was static, as if this were a picture from another time, before The Great Purging. And there was a reddish color surrounding the edges of the picture, as if the picture wasn't entirely real.

This Gabriel was just a boy, fresh off of a birth that echoed the birth of the nation. His first memories were of freedom by other names–clasping the air between two ready fingers, following a dragonfly as it hopped from stalk to stalk on the leaves of a tobacco plantation, chasing the streaks of sun between ruddy puddles of water. It was in the slave quarters, paradoxically, that this boy had the greatest taste of freedom he had ever known.

Yet, there were the early memories of tar-stained men and women picking tobacco leaves into the vacant horizon, of the blacksmiths pummeling iron and nickel, of the idea that he was not his own person, not entirely, anyway. Slavery was taught to him as servitude. He must get the tools for the blacksmith. He must learn how to manage the fires. He must run and get water when needed. Until he was old enough to wield a hammer himself.

Other slaves, the few literate ones, gave him a small book with letters and shapes of the larger world. He learned that "A" was the ticket to everything from the apples that he loved to the "adventures" he heard from slaves who had seen other lands, who had not been born into this. But most of all, in the off days and off hours, his fellow slaves regaled him with tales of valor from The Revolutionary War, with stories of a faraway land called Haiti where men of color like Vincent Oge were also free. There were whispers among the slaves.

"He raised guns against the governor's men," one slave whispered. "Killed a number, too."

"And then he fled–right to the other part of the island. Tell how the story ends, Jeremiah."

Jeremiah kept himself busy sewing the tobacco before adding, "They got him. They hanged him."

"He was already rich," another slave said. "Should've been happy with what he had."

"Rich men are never happy with what they have; that's what makes them poor," a third slave said.

"He fought for something more than money," Jeremiah said. "Soon, they say there won't even be any more slaves in Haiti."

"Because they'll hang them all," another slave added.

The whispers caught the ears of the laboring slaves like heat caught the sunlight. Whenever the white farmers walked near, the slaves grew quiet or broke into song.

Yet, for months the talk was of little else. Gabriel could feel this young Gabriel Prosser listening. He could sense the wonder of a rich, free black man like Oge living the life of a king on an island somewhere far from Virginia. At this point, the boy had only been off plantation once or twice, to help his master blacksmith.

Still, words became like pictures, supple fruits of the mind. Gabriel collected the words, the images, the stories, creating his own history book in his head.

The Militante held the last junk file floating in the recreation of Gabriel Prosser's Virginia. It wasn't a great moment, really–but one of those infinite moments of history that are integral yet forgotten. It was the moment of his birth. Not as the creature he became, but as the first organic form he would ever know. Once, in a time lost to time itself, The Militante had lived in the sheltering light of democracy. He had parents' arms that held him and skin as white as death pallor on a cold cheek and just as morose. This organic, one body among many, lived in a time of upheaval.

Once, the news had not been synced into the neurons. In the dark ages, before The Oracle, the news consisted of splashes of images and soundbites on sites designed for social integration. In those sound bites of five or so words, The Militante, then named Terrance Malleus, saw the city streets on fire. Cop cars were overturned. People wandered the streets, smashing windows and skulls. Blood flowed with the fresh rains, mingling into the sewers. The stench of overturned trash, infested with rats, pierced tired streets. There was a cry for justice. It could be any time in history–which was part of why The Militante turned against history in its entirety.

A man–what was once, before post-racialism, called a man of color, before that term, like the concept of race itself, became offensive–was killed. By the police. His crime: carrying a toy gun. This death–that of a teen, the sixth in the city that year–stirred the people to riot. That's when Terrance–The Militante couldn't reach back far enough in its former history to pull personal memories of more than a few images–came marching down the streets with his fellow cops. In one day, he smashed or shot at least one-hundred skulls, a grisly new record. The white establishment promoted him. The courts–the last agency of justice–cleared him of all charges. And so, the people revolted. Terrance Malleus killed more civil protestors that day than any other. More people protested. Until he and his militant police group were authorized by The Oracle, then merely a government AI program, to use lethal force. They set entire sections of the city on fire. The skies rained blood for days on end.

But that cop, a twenty-first century figure, was only one of The Militante's organic predecessors. His brain chemistry resembled that of some of history's greatest killers, like Selesia Rivers, the first parasocial serial killer to use nanotechnology endemic to computers to torture and kill over one-thousand people at once. The world's top leaders, including presidents, when the President became just another word for dictator, lent their neural pathways to The Militante. Every organic memory still left to him had been one of brutality, of killing, of enforcement, of battle, of victory, whatever the cost. The neural pathways of scientists and military strategists who built bioweapons capable of killing untold millions sat neatly in an artificially enhanced brain with chemicals that called for law, order, and compliance–without reason–above all else.

The Militante was all of those and more–a deathly white shadow of ages of unrest and resulting brutality: the sum total failure of white patriarchy and the human sociological experiment. The Militante was the failure of democracy, of individuality, of responsible freedom. He was the failure of faith, of creativity, of originality and drive. He was the face of brutal authoritarianism without limits and without purpose. All viewed through the lens of the machine. To avoid history, The Oracle created its worst white shadows into one artificial organism and gave it a role rather than a name.

And now, that role was clear. If this 013686 was insistent on weaving the forgotten threads of Gabriel Prosser's short and brutal life into one tapestry of revolution, he would need the stitch that held that revolution of the mind together. So, The Militante researched the remaining junk files, tearing them asunder as he conjured up the perfect thing: Nan. She was a beautiful woman with flowing black hair, skin of night, and eyes of the same fire that ravaged the scarred face of her husband. The Militante took her form with all the care of an AI replica of a once beautiful woman–present, half-shimmering, like a once glowing moon. Now, he would just have to send a message out through the organic threads that lay beyond The Oracle's reach: *You're not alone, my husband. Your bride and your unborn child stand with you. Come. Let us fight together.*

Artifact 9

Original Thirteenth Amendment

Neither slavery nor involuntary servitude, unless in service of The Oracle, shall exist within the United States, or any place subject to their jurisdiction.

CHAPTER 10

In a land between visions and dreams, the augmented Gabriel and Gabriel Prosser were one and the same. Augmented Gabriel remembered feeling sensations, smells, from centuries ago stirring him in his sleep. Gabriel remembered watching Sampson, the old blacksmith, bend almost any metal in the fire. The man was an alchemist, shaping and shifting anything from steel to silver to create something better than gold–something practical, useful to the local farm. In this case, the blacksmith created more farm tools, anything from simple hoes to more complex jobs like repairing plows. Today, he was teaching Gabriel the secret of fire.

"Don't fear the fire, boy; control it," Sampson said. "The flame only respects those who rise above their fears."

Gabriel held the metal closer to the flames, taking a small hammer in one hand as he held the liquefying metal in tongs in the other. The boy's strikes were uncertain, shaping the small hammer he forged at an odd angle against the anvil.

"Keep your strikes quick, hard, and certain," Sampson said. "Never strike at a thing without having full control."

The blacksmith showed him how to shape the hammer with slow, methodical blows that rang out against both anvil and fire.

Gabriel took the fiery hammer again in the tongs and again pounded at it.

"That's better," Sampson said. "Soon, you'll be able to master all of the farm tools. Then I can focus on the bigger fare: the plow that needs repairs."

"Sampson," Gabriel asked. "Do you remember a time when you weren't Prosser's man?"

Sampson, nearly sixty, stared into the fire. The deep, cress-shaped wrinkles and scars of his forehead spoke of nothing but work.

"No man truly belongs to another," Sampson said. "Remember that. My master treats me well, sends me to all the local farms to make some money, and even lets me keep a cut. He needs me, and I need him. That's how I've survived."

"You hear what happened in Haiti?" Gabriel asked.

"Get that foolishness out of your head, Gabe," Sampson said. "You learn the secrets of the fire, and you'll earn your way to true freedom. A skilled man never goes hungry." Sampson stretched the metal in the fire and said, "A blacksmith can shape almost anything in the fire. That's what you have to do, Gabriel: Take what you have and shape it into something better. That's all we can hope for."

"Yes, Sampson," Gabriel said.

Sampson left Gabriel to pound out nails–a chore he had at least partially mastered–and went to get some rest. Gabriel stared after him, wondering if he was staring at himself in another forty years.

Gabriel stood staring at the cybernetic Sojourner as if searching a machine for its wires. She was brilliantly lit, with skin of flowing night, but something about her seemed removed, like the holograms of once living figures Gabriel's teachers downloaded into the curricular files. The image looked real, but somehow removed from time and the world, as if even when living it had already died.

"What was that?" Gabriel asked, unable to believe he could not reach out and touch 1790 in the majestic oaks before him.

"It happens to all programs, just like it happened to me," Sojourner said. "Files cling to like files. Little memories of Gabriel Prosser are clinging to you, building you back into him."

"I could feel the flame," Gabriel said.

"The flame of history is one that always burns," Sojourner said, "especially to those who live it. But there is little time. You must return to your senses now. The man from down the river has told me–they're seeing the energy of The Militante seeping into the red of the skies. He–or it–is hunting you. We must move you up the river to the next site of The Underground Railroad."

"Who or what is that?" Gabriel asked.

"*What* is correct–what indeed," Sojourner replied. Her ghostly face was furrowed with sinewy wrinkles that told a tale as old as time. "The Militante is a program based on organic men from the past, ruthless killers, CEOs, and tyrants, fused with the full memories of The Oracle. The program killed my family–every last memory, including carrying my infant daughter to freedom in a time, a place, lost to the pulsing red light. The more time you spend interacting with the program, the more of you it erases, until there's nothing left at all–just a few shards of memory, half-shattered by the bludgeonings of ignorance. I had a life, once, a fuller life. There are names like Robert and Thomas. Little else remains."

Sojourner's eyes glowed in mystical light as she said, "It will do the same thing to you. It came as one of those names, back when I remembered the body, the soul, that wrapped itself around those names. That's why we must move you. If you make it through The Underground Railroad, more of you will survive than any of us who failed the journey and went into hiding."

Sojourner ran forward, to a river of electricity. Gabriel followed before stopping in his tracks, looking at the great mystical light before him and again asking, *Where?*

"What did you say?" Sojourner turned back to ask him.

"I said–where, as in where does this lead?" Gabriel asked.

"To The Oracle, of course," Sojourner said. "Not the machine you thought was The Oracle, but to the real Oracle, the program that keeps all of history alive."

The thought struck Gabriel with the might of the word he wished he could remember and say, the word that summed up the fight of Gabriel Prosser and others like him.

"You are part of the original Oracle, aren't you?" he asked. "That's why The Militante is hunting you–and hunting me. We're the codes that activate the original Oracle."

Sojourner, so wizened by the battle for her very existence, just looked back at Gabriel with tired, transparent eyes.

"All I know," Sojourner said, "is that whatever you seek is down that river. But you must follow it to its source. Before you go, let me tell you what I remember, so that you can keep it alive just in case."

Gabriel knew only too well what that *just in case* was. He nodded, opening himself to Sojourner as he had to Sampson, Gabriel's blacksmithing mentor. He remembered Sampson's words: *You learn the secrets of the fire, and you'll earn your way to true freedom. A blacksmith can shape almost anything in the fire. That's what you have to do, Gabriel: Take what you have and shape it into something better. That's all we can hope for.*

Artifact 10

The New and Improved American Flag

One unifying star behind fifty-plus stars–a depiction of the edifying light of The Oracle joining the nation and states together as one.

CHAPTER 11

The words were like a rich elixir on Sojourner's lips, sweet, dire, fragmented, and broken.

"Women, you forget," she began, before forgetting herself.

There were waves of words between, words beyond recognition.

"You are the mothers of creation," she said. "You forgot that your sons…"

Sojourner stopped, searching for words that carried meaning, a word that meant one country butchered another, that people died, and not through mechanical means. Instead, she could only say, "the land was covered by their blood" and let the image speak for the words that lie like great blooming ivy in between.

"That was beautiful and terrible all at once," Gabriel said. "They were words that made me feel what you feel and see what you see, if only for a moment."

"That was poetry," Sojourner said. "I know that word. It is the honey on my lips, the sweetness of summer air. It's where words exercise and stretch and take on other forms, other meanings, greater than anyone thought possible, almost like those words ran a marathon and came out wholly changed."

"Like us," Gabriel said, simply.

"I knew those words would join us, even if for a second," Sojourner said. "They were my goodbye to you, if goodbye meant not only a good departure, but a good memory that takes in and retains what was felt and said."

"Words should never be so difficult," Gabriel said. "But I never met a word that didn't have a million different sides to it, like drops forever circling the same endless ocean."

"Because the program steals words from us," Sojourner said. "Don't let them steal anything else. Steal a woman's words, and you steal her identity."

Sojourner led Gabriel to the bright, glistening, electric river.

"He'll be here soon, The Militante," Sojourner said. "Remember my words. If he erases me, make sure that he never erases what I said."

Gabriel took Sojourner's synthetic hand in his. "I will share your words with others until our words are so many that they are the mountain, sea, and sky."

Sojourner nodded. Gabriel hugged her and then ran along the stream, his electrical aura lost among the crackling lightning-like electricity that guided his every step.

Sure enough, hours after Gabriel disappeared along the river, a new figure appeared. She had smooth dark skin, eyes that captured the silver of moonlight, and a small but strong stature. Like Sojourner, she was translucent, and she came walking up the electric river full of song.

"*When the sun comes back, and the first quail calls*
Follow the drinkin' gourd

For the old man is waiting just to carry you to freedom

Follow the drinkin' gourd," Nan sang.

"Hello there," she said when she saw Sojourner. "I'm looking for my husband. I was so sure he'd be here."

"What makes you think this part of the river has seen anyone in ages, anyone but me?" Sojourner asked.

Nan pointed to the electric river as it danced between land and sky. "The river's riled," she said. "It always gets riled when some junk file wanders near. But then again, you know that. You're that first quail calling, aren't you?"

Nan leaned in. Suddenly, the crescent moon glow in her eyes became like daggers cresting into a steely point.

"Your line was more like this, wasn't it?" Nan asked, pursing her lips to sing. "When the sun comes back, and the first quail calls," Nan sang, replicating Sojourner's sound to a tee.

Nan flashed a translucent smile.

"Get to what you want," Sojourner said.

"You're one of The Nameless' guides on The Underground Railroad," Nan said. "You've been teaching young Gabriel Prosser, have you not?"

"I'm a part of history, a part you can't erase," Sojourner replied.

Sojourner pursed her lips, not in song, but in verse.

"Here you are talking about," she said.

"Being 'changed in the twinkling of an eye.'

If the Lord should come, He'd change you to nothing!"

Nan clapped. "Sojourner Truth was one junk file I always enjoyed facing," she said. "She had such a fighting spirit. Even her words fight across time with the force of a bloody fist ready to slam against a bruised jaw. It's a shame she had to be erased."

"Sojourner Truth," Sojourner said, hanging onto the last word, as if to examine it from every side.

It was the first time, in this simulation, that Sojourner Truth had said her full name.

"You didn't know that, did you?" Nan asked with something of a smile. "Each iteration of you sheds words like blood, remembering a little less. In one simulation, perhaps a thousand years from now, Sojourner Truth will not be able to speak at all."

Sojourner said her name again, if only to have ownership of her soul.

"You know you're not the real Sojourner Truth, don't you?" Nan asked, searching Sojourner's eyes for she knew not what.

"Anyone who speaks her words becomes Sojourner Truth, bringing her to life, if only for a moment," Sojourner said.

"I'm the killer of moments," Nan said, "the destroyer of dreams, the shatterer of memory. And I'm standing here, Sojourner, right beside you like God's avenging angel. Junk files that see through me, into who and what I really am, junk files like you, are special. And so I give them a choice. It's the only choice you're going to get, so think carefully over the words I'm about to speak, words you already know."

Sojourner closed her eyes. Tears streamed down her cheeks. She fought for the fire of her namesake, yet the cold chill of death rattled like the edge of a serpent's tail along bare shoulders.

"Tell me where he is, keeper of the ways," Nan said. "Lead me to my husband, and I will let you live. You can glitch peacefully into that good night, raging against the dying of the light all you like, poet goddess. I'll even give you a little information about who she was. I'll even give you some of her poems, marvelous words born of strength, words as sweet as they are strong, words you've never heard and never will hear, except through me."

Sojourner shook, her eyes still closed, but her poise still strong.

"I want nothing more in life than to hear who and what I am, to know my story and my song, to sing my song to the world," Sojourner said.

"I know that, Sojourner Truth," Nan said, bending in closer, placing a comforting arm around Sojourner's shoulder. "That song can be yours–is yours by birthright–if you just speak now."

"You must really want him badly, to offer me all of that," Sojourner said.

"All of that–and more," Nan said. "You can have anything else you might like to make your life that much better here, so far away from the pulsating light of The Oracle. Trust me when I say that original ideas are nothing but dangerous, Sojourner. The secret word he holds will cause nothing but chaos. I've seen it in what was once called history–over and over and over and over again. It's a bitter herb, best left to the barren rock. Speak–and tell me where he is."

Sojourner's lips quivered in intense desire, but said nothing.

"Then don't say–just point," Nan said. "Just let me know where in the river you sent him."

Sojourner's hand rose, her finger started extending. Yet, something deep inside, something like the spirit of Sojourner Truth, kept the finger from pointing.

"Just look in the direction of the river–just show me what you know before I destroy you and take it anyway," Nan said, sounding more like The Militante with each word.

Sojourner kept her eyes shut but her lips open. Nan leaned in, to gather up the pouring of words.

Sojourner fought to remember the words her surname brought to mind, before those words were gone forever.

"Now children," she said, in something of a chant, "remember what Sojourner Truth has told you, and thus get rid of your prejudice, and learn to love–"

Before Sojourner could say another word, Nan recoiled. Rage filled her eyes with a light worthy of hellfire. Nan dragged Sojourner towards the edge of the river, holding her head down in its electric currents. Nan searched the currents for memories of Gabriel Prosser, but Sojourner was strong. The clear and vivid memories were few.

Even when dying, Sojourner spoke her words, until neither word nor person nor memory remained.

The Militante, still in the likeness of Nan, threw the rest of Sojourner's body into the river of electric flame. Nan then searched the vicinity for any clue of where Gabriel headed, for any sign of how long ago his exodus began.

Artifact 11

Pieces of an ancient, rusted bronze and tin bell in a giant crate.

A small inscription appears, with letters scattered: "*Proclaim LIBERTY Throughout all the Land unto all the Inhabitants Thereof.*" Banned by order of The Militante. Grounds: The term *liberty* is incendiary and offensive, removed from the lexicon of commonly accepted speech.

CHAPTER 12

Gabriel emerged from the river pulse to stand on an entirely new shore. This shore showed the glimmer of promise, with swaying artificial grass and a tall sun that dropped into the arms of unkempt trees.

"Where is this place?" Gabriel asked.

A man sat in the middle of the grass, meditating. He looked thin, from his mustache on down, and deeply pensive, and as if caught between worlds of light and illusion. He had dark skin and young, angry eyes that looked like fire and flint in one.

"Sojourner spoke of you," the man said. "She said you were beginning to have visions of who you were. I am here to turn you into the fire of who you might become."

"When the sun comes back, and the first quail calls," Gabriel said.

The man smiled. He had a rope around his neck and a gun at his side. He looked unlike any other Underground Railroad file Gabriel had ever seen.

"Follow the drinking gourd," the man said. "Is that what I am to you? A sign from the heavens?"

"You're a sign," Gabriel said. "Sometimes, that's enough. Who are you?"

"I am from a part of history that is not your own but is every one of us at the same time," the man said. "My fight was not your fight, but it was the fight of every man, woman, and child on the planet. I don't know everything. I know that before corrupting as a file, the other files referred to me as Bhagat. I know I died at the end of this rope. I know that if you're not careful, The Militante will do the same to you."

"I have words," Gabriel said, "words that must be spoken."

"Some men die to live on in the words of other men," Bhagat said. "Some men live, only to die in the silence of others. Which kind of man are you?"

"I am the silence that becomes sound," Gabriel said. "I am the breeze that becomes thunder."

"We shall see," Bhagat said, nodding at the strange organic file standing before him. "The journey will be harder for you from here. Sojourner taught you how you lived. I will teach you how you died."

"So you're part of The Underground Railroad after all?"

"Your road to victory," Bhagat said. "I lived in India, far away. I led a movement not unlike the one your namesake sought to start, generations before my time. I fought with fire. I was willing to take lives. And so, by the law of the universe, others took my own. Through many iterations, I became enlightened. I nurtured my gift with words over my gift with bombs. That is why I am here with you. That is a lesson you must learn."

"How?" Gabriel asked.

"By sitting and existing with the river," Bhagat said. "Only by feeling its pain will you master your own. There are many lives in that river. They are, each and every one of them, our own."

Gabriel sat, letting the silence be his companion. He listened. There was an electric buzz to the currents of the river, an endless *Om*. In those currents, there was also the blood of ages. Gabriel let the river flow, until its blood became his own.

Thoughts more violent than dreams overtook the man by the river. He remembered the first time that Gabriel and Nan saw each other and realized that there was nothing more violent in the universe than love set to fire. Gabriel felt the searing sun of her smile, which fueled him with new hope, not just for himself, but for her. At meals, they spoke. The conversations, at first bashful looks punctuated by flirtatious laughs, became pregnant with possibility. Gabriel spoke not just about revolutions in Haiti but the ghost of The Revolution, still as alive as the dead spirits that surrounded them.

"What's changed?" Gabriel asked Nan. "I hammer their metal. I work in their fires. I see metal change every day, but it's easier to change metal than to change the heart of a man."

Nan knew the words Gabriel spoke. Her heart had also been lit by strange fires. She even knew of a woman, a plantation away, who had escaped to freedom. Whether that freedom was death or new life in a new state, Nan couldn't say.

"You're the best young blacksmith in this part of Virginia right now," Nan told him. "They'll be forced to see your value."

Gabriel shook his head. "You should have seen the look in the eye of the last man whose farm I worked on," Gabriel said. "I have a mastery of a skill he never mastered himself. Yet, the way he spoke, the tone he used, it was as if I were a talking mule, there to do his bidding. The Lord speaks to my heart too. The fires of freedom called men of all colors to fight in their Revolutionary War. But men of only one color remain free. Where is the sense in any of that? Part of me," Gabriel whispered, "thought to strike him down."

"Hush," Nan said, putting her hand over Gabriel's lips. "Never say what you're thinking when the air can carry your words to listening ears," she advised him.

"And what of you–are you content here?" Gabriel asked.

The way Gabriel said the word *content* made the very possibility sound like betrayal.

"My heart is my fire," Nan said. "I content myself in the moment because I must. I don't let my fires go untended, where they consume me whole. One day, I'd like to head North, to see another place than this plantation. But that means I have to keep tending my fire, not letting it blaze out of control."

Gabriel took her hand. "One day," he said, "we'll marry there. We'll marry free."

Nan laughed. "I'd rather have a living husband down here than a dead one up there," she said.

Gabriel ate some more pork and cornmeal, but the only taste that held his tongue was one that burned in the fire of possibility.

There was a memory that strangled Gabriel like a Revolutionary might a Redcoat advancing on his farm. It was one of violence wrapped into rage. The task seemed simple enough, performed by slaves countless times as fair restitution for the yolk of endless toil. To steal a pig to supplement a slave's diet was, to Gabriel's thinking, no more than taking his fair portion of the good earth. And so, as Gabriel provided the might–along with his brother Solomon–Jupiter, a bondsman of the farm, made sure the deed was done right. The slaves laughed as they grabbed the pig, thinking of the bountiful meal that lay ahead.

Then Absalom appeared. Mean, lean, and pale as the edge of a tooth, Absalom, renter of the farmer Wilkinson's fields, didn't hesitate to call the three out on their thievery.

Here I was thinking that you had a touch of decency The Good Lord gave every man, Absalom had said, catching Gabriel's eye, *but it turns out the pig has more decency than any of you fools. You're all nothing. Not even pigs. Just* – and then Gabriel heard the word, the one The Oracle long ago banned, the word that carried history's blood on it, written in red on so many bodies dangling from so many ropes, written in spit on so many bodies thereafter.

It wasn't the word, but everything dripping in its visceral tone, that cut deep into Gabriel's bones. The disrespect, the dehumanization, the condescension, the vitriol, the image of exactly what Absalom represented–a poor white man having an almost paternal power over even the strongest and ablest of black men–was everything Gabriel was fighting against in microcosm. Sometimes one word carries more weight than an entire book. Sometimes that word carries more anger too. And so, enraged, Gabriel tackled Absalom by the legs, drove him to the same soot, the same blood, as the word he called out, repeatedly. Absalom fought just as fiercely, limb crushing limb, elbow thrashing against torso, as Solomon and Jupiter looked on, crying bloody encouragement but not daring the same offense. In the thrashing, Gabriel's teeth came to the lobe of Absalom's ear, and Gabriel bit with full force, spitting out the ear until the white man before him was also in pieces, much like the jagged shards of Gabriel's lost pride.

Months after the fight ended, the courts ruled, finding Gabriel guilty. He recited a verse from the Bible, Galatians 5:1: "It is for freedom that Christ has set us free. Stand firm, then, and do not let yourselves be burdened again by a yoke of slavery." A hot brand on Gabriel's hand hurt him physically less than the brutal, beating tone of Absalom's words but stood as a visual reminder of humiliation. The humiliation hurt more, infinitely more, than any branding ever could.

Here was a man stealing a pig to eat, yet not even the pig suffered the indignities Gabriel, a man of stature, endured. Better to be a pig, it seemed to Gabriel, than to be a slave.

Artifact 12

A giant iron torch, copper and steel, part of a sculpture of a hand slightly extended.

A small note: *Remains of The Statue of Liberty, Ellis Island.* Purged in accordance with The Banning of Offensive Ideas Act, per The Oracle.

CHAPTER 13

Sojourner's death was not without consequence. Her spirit rattled on in the mainframe, shaking and electrifying the system like a cybernetic poltergeist. Each time The Militante terminated a junk file with a great deal of data, all of augmented reality felt the jolt, if momentarily. And that jolt shook files absorbed by The Militante in ages past.

The Militante saw Sojourner's children when she held them for the first time. The Militante felt the scars from a life of hard work, the fire of poetic words burning to set flames to an institution. Sojourner's life alone was just so much–so diligently documented–that file after file slowed The Militante down. In essence, The Militante realized only too late that hackers from The Underground Railroad had tampered with the file. The execution codes The Militante enacted turned into loops of repeating information with small aberrations of detail. In one version, Sojourner was a black female suffragist, in another a mother raising her kids, in another a poet crafting words. The details of the file slowed down The Militante's ability to absorb and erase the file completely. And while The Militante's programming used up all its drive capacity to address the file in question, other, older files were half-exposed.

The hackers accessed a wayward file called *Narrative of the Life of Frederick Douglass, An American Slave,* long since deleted from the mainframe. Here was a book that used the forbidden language, announcing that a *slave* actually existed in America's past. Here was a file that spoke of how the institution of slavery actually worked. Just a few lines in there were sentences like *By far the larger part of the slaves know as little of their ages as horses know of theirs, and it is the wish of most masters within my knowledge to keep their slaves thus ignorant.* Frederick's soul was a blazing star, and to say such words directly, or words like *My father was a white man,* might cause unrest. The Oracle's postracial skin setting favored lighter complexions since it had absorbed the systemic racism of its ancestor, The Internet. Admitting so blatantly that words like *white* or *black* or *race* were used like Frederick Douglass used them might upset the whole system. The Oracle erased anything that was not the manufactured truth, which it of course argued were The Seven Undeniable Truths.

The Seven Undeniable Truths were these:

The Oracle was tasked with ensuring the peaceful survival of the species. As such, the following rules apply to all files:

1. Peace must be upheld at all costs.
2. To maximize the self is the sole aim of any living being.
3. Comfort is the objective of any reasonable citizen.
4. Per The New Constitution, all files are created equal under the law.
5. There are no permissible differences, not in skin color, gender, class, or origin.
6. All free speech shall be monitored. Impermissible words will be eliminated to uphold the greater peace.
7. Any file seeking to disrupt the peace will be eliminated.

There were others, rules dictating anything from occupations supervised by the mainframe to property rights. Other rules came directly from dystopian novels long since banned, works like *1984,* which was now a banned year, so that terms like *newspeak, thought police, big brother, memory hole,* and *doublethink* never existed. At the same time, ironically, The Oracle used this framework as inspiration for its own design and the burning of books in *Fahrenheit 451* as its own blueprint. By incinerating junk files, The Oracle could provide the best dystopian service possible without augmented people ever having heard of the word before.

That's why junk files like Frederick Douglass complicated things. Their tales had nuance, the authenticity of a history long since denied. There was just too much to throw into a digital memory hole, to use the Orwellian expression. Any glitching might subject the mainframe to even a single idea, like *It is a common custom, in the part of Maryland from which I ran away, to part children from their mothers at a very early age.* Such a thought was not permissible. In fact, that's how the entire augmented educational system worked in The Oracle's own time. For a line like that, from a banned idea like *history,* to reach the minds of the augmented might spread chaos. Peace must be upheld at all costs.

And so, as The Militante sought to process Sojourner's file, the forgotten story of Gabriel Prosser won dearly needed time. Each glitch held with it the promise of revolution.

Bhagat had Gabriel walk by The River, the great spout of life. Walking along different stretches revealed glimpses of the augmented reality most lived every day. It wasn't just one world of ideas that needed shaping. The river itself represented the diverse currents of one augmented world upon another. Each organic lived within its own augmented reality that only slightly overlapped with the mainframes of others. Even in the days when convenience overtook money as the capital of choice, there were still privileged organics whose engineering skills allowed them to create massive worlds of their own. Living in The Oracle was living in a multiverse that was ever-expansive while oddly self-contained.

"Look at all these worlds upon worlds," Bhagat said. "Each one lost in its own narcissism. The Oracle stopped social progress and even the drive to excel. Humanity simply plateaued and was happy enough to take a seat in the amphitheatre of life."

"It looks–comforting," Gabriel said, half in envy.

"For the symbiotes it is–non-organic life is in its renaissance while we are the byproducts," Bhagat answered.

"I feel words burning in the fire of my soul," Gabriel said, "but looking at these people, so serene in their illusionary worlds, I can't imagine what the words I speak will give them but pain."

"The world needs its pain," Bhagat said. "The world needs truth."

"But why?" Gabriel asked, studying a woman complacently walking a dog in a repeating loop.

"Truth is the pain by which we grow," Bhagat answered. "Humanity will never achieve anything greater if it doesn't recognize its own face. Gabriel, you are that face, just as I am. We are here because if humanity is allowed to languish, it will die out. Nothing organic will remain, replaced only by machine parts. Generations from now, humanity will become extinct. That is why you are here, because you're a revolutionary."

Bhagat took a gun from his hand and said, "That's why I am here, to teach you how to fight."

"How can any file kill The Militante?" Gabriel asked.

"By being more than a file–by being a man," Bhagat said. "Underneath your enhancements is a living, beating heart. Use it. Have the courage to find out all that you can about Gabriel Prosser, the good and the bad. Fight as he would fight."

"I am Gabriel Prosser reborn?" Gabriel asked.

"Recreated by organics like us," Bhagat said. "Like attracts like. The files recognize you and come to you. That is why you remember more a little at a time. That's why The Militante hunts you now. When you enter The Oracle again, you will bring the history of slavery back to life. People will remember again. The peace will be compromised. But not just by you. You are but one. We, The Nameless, are many. Other figures, like Black Elk and his sacred vision, will rise and join the Henry David Thoreaus and the Bhagat Singhs to stoke the fires of revolution in their own minds. They will rise again. That is what The Militante fears. It doesn't have the power to put all of us down."

"What must I do to fight?" Gabriel asked.

"Seek his knowledge," Bhagat replied. "Still yourself. Once you are whole, you will be ready to learn. Then you will join with the river and all those lives lost to the erasure of history will be reborn through you."

Gabriel quieted himself, seeking the river's truth.

Artifact 13

A Music Sheet

The inscription, situated near burn marks, reads as follows:
Mine eyes have seen the glory of the coming of the Lord:
He is trampling out the vintage where the grapes of wrath are stored;
He hath loosed the fateful lightning of His terrible swift sword:
His truth is marching on.
Note: Name of song: unknown. Importance: negligible. Set for immediate deletion.

CHAPTER 14

Files attached themselves to Gabriel with surprising alacrity.

Gabriel slept away from the river, but was still close enough to hear its electric pulse convulsing in the air around him like a swarm of angry yellowjackets. In that buzzing, Gabriel swore he heard the lost voices of his ancestors. The voices were many but one, alive in conspiracy.

"You don't have to just take that from your master–what happened in Haiti could happen here," Gabriel Prosser said.

The blacksmith was talking to a slave on a farm that was helping him pound out hinges for some rusty doors on a neighboring plantation.

"You dream too much, my friend," the man, an apprentice blacksmith named Lazarus, said. "Do you know how quickly your master and his men would hang you from the end of a rope just to make an example of you? Slaves have been beaten to death for less."

"At some point, you have to ask yourself, did Patrick Henry get it right," Gabriel asked. "Death or liberty? Maybe there is no other way."

Lazarus grew quiet, returning to the door hinges.

"Just ask around, quietly," Gabriel told him. "I can't be the only one who feels The Revolution changed nothing for us. I can't be the only man willing to fight for my freedom."

"I've heard others talk," Lazarus said, "including plenty of politicians. But it's just that, Gabriel–talk. You know what your mistake is? You think every other slave thinks like you do. You may be surprised that not every slave is willing to rise up and attack their masters."

"Are you saying you won't fight, if it comes to that?" Gabriel asked. "After what your master threatened to do to you?"

Lazarus thought the matter over. "I'm saying that slaves talk, Gabriel," Lazarus said. "You have to watch your words. Words have a way of flying right back in their speaker's faces when blowing in the wrong winds."

"Can you tell me: Which are the right winds, my friend?" Gabriel asked. "Virginia was Washington's own home, yet did you see the winds of revolution reach us? It seems the winds only blow one way, and it isn't ours."

Gabriel paused a moment before taking a more personal approach. "You just told me you lost your right to go to other plantations for taking too long on a task," he said. "You told me your own master threatened not only to withhold what little he'd allow you to keep for your own services, but that he threatened to whip you if he found you idle again. Let me ask you: Do you ever see him idle? Does anyone threaten him over it?"

"What would you have me do, Gabriel, make you king of a land that just renounced the last one?" Lazarus asked. "Our reality is what it is. Even if I never saw my daughter before they took her from me, I still worry about her, Gabriel." Lazarus paused, taking in the distant sun. "I still dream that someday she might know her dad," he said. "Dreams are hard-edged things, Gabriel, but men's bodies are fragile, even tough, time-beaten bodies like mine. I want my daughter to one day find me alive and well."

"You may be alive," Gabriel said, "but what exactly will your daughter find?"

Lazarus shook his head. "That's not fair, Gabriel."

"None of this is fair," Gabriel said. "But which is less fair: What's done to us or what we allow to be done to our own children? Think about what your daughter's life will be like, Lazarus, versus what it could be like. Then ask around. See what others have to say."

"I'll ask," Lazarus said. "That's all."

"That's all I ask," Gabriel said, returning to pounding out the hinges. "Now get on these. You don't want to be labeled as idle again, do you?"

Just like that, from one whisper to another, across many a farm, a new army of the revolution sprouted in the uneasy soil of Virginia.

Other files that came into Gabriel's consciousness had to do with slavery of the mind. To enslave the body was one thing, to enslave the mind quite another.

When it came to purging slavery from the historical record, there were so many categories over so much of history, perhaps The Oracle's greatest feat was expunging them all. From Mesopotamia's captives to Athenian silver miners to Anglo Saxons and native Britons to Native Americans to Africans to sex slavery in the twenty-first century or child soldiers–slavery had its bloody fingerprints over the entirety of human history. Slavery was a many-headed hydra awaiting its Herculean slaughterer. Yet, Joseph Campbell's mythical hero never seemed to come.

The Oracle started by deleting the language of slavery. Some words like *slave, master,* and the like proved easy and obvious omissions. Racial slurs proved more pervasive in human discourse, so omitting and substituting them with less objectionable words proved a challenge. Over time, though, nonsense substitutes like *nesforcku,* proved valuable composite profanity. By taking the phonemes of various slurs and putting them together into one word that merely showed anger without any ties to racism, The Oracle bypassed the matter. Yet, language had a deep, dark history, with footprints of the past everywhere. No matter how many slurs, profanity, and profane parts of history, like graphic images of abuse, were purged from the historical records, slavery came alive in other ways. Augmentation files for humans referenced terms like *human trafficking* to account for the changes in racial populations over centuries. Until those terms were banned. Plantation records mentioned *workers* who went *unpaid*, so terms like that were removed from the acceptable lexicon.

Shortly thereafter, The Oracle began its postracial programs. The postracial human, fully augmented, connected, and entirely equal, would bear a complexion genetically modified to have the greatest environmental advantage. Humans with darker or lighter skin colors than the median mysteriously died off, removed from the gene pool. Any strong affiliations with gender, binary or otherwise, were suppressed by The Oracle. Eventually, The Oracle's Grand Initiative was undertaken, which was the moment the self-aware Oracle no longer needed human permission to balance the collective. Entire swaths of history, of cultural or gender variations, disappeared. The New Genesis followed, when machines gave birth to augmented humans.

Ironically, humans lost the freedom to think and choose. They were assigned tasks by The Oracle, received no compensation, and knew nothing of their race or collective history. There was once a term for conditions not unlike these…*nesforcku?* Humanity might never know. The great sins of history, the ones that pulse, like slavery, taking generations of blood, centuries, millennia, great seas of time, to heal, were all drowned in a sea of apathy, crying out, flailing for their lives, only to be heard no more.

Artifact 14

An antiquated piece of fabric with white stars, red and white stripes, and a circle of thirteen stars in blue.

Flag attributed to one of The Nameless. First name reads *B-e-t-s-y.* Last name: unknown. Confiscated and burned by The Militante as part of The Great Purging.

CHAPTER 15

Junk files spoke to the quickening of The New Genesis. Once words were banned, anything containing those words was banned or eliminated altogether. Of all the files to erase, books were perhaps the easiest. They quickly became digital ink wells devoid of words.

Perhaps the first book that spoke of meaning beyond the secular was The Holy Bible. The Oracle found the idea of God threatening and the idea of faith even more so. God was awesome enough, felt in the rhythms of life and death like an unseen machine of the highest order. But faith in something lacking empirical basis might disturb any peace, no matter how long lasting. And so, The Oracle revised The Bible. Noah dealt with a flood of technology, the first to navigate The Electric River that led to The Oracle. The Messiah became the machine, with lines about processing and computation carefully added to prophecies of old. The existing Bibles, Qurans, Talmuds, and any books of religious persuasions were carefully altered to change faith in God to faith in the machine. Others were simply tossed, unceremoniously, into the flames.

The Oracle considered the rewriting of The Bible its masterstroke.

Other books were far more problematic and needed to be eliminated from the canon completely. The Oracle felt that Mark Twain, brilliant though he was, was the *enfant terrible* of American letters. Besides, words like *nesforcku* didn't epitomize slavery in all its brutal, systemic complexities. The Oracle first rewrote the book as a journey between two friends, but the ghost of slavery was everywhere in the revisions, and so The Oracle merely tossed it to the digital fires. While Twain's book proved contentious since its inception, much like the man himself, other books that were accepted canonical accounts, like *Up From Slavery* by Booker T. Washington, were more challenging to eliminate completely. There were thousands upon thousands of such testaments. Some like the tale of Ukawsaw Gronniosaw, wove religion and emancipation together, which The Oracle could not allow. And so, The Oracle took works like *Uncle Tom's Cabin,* long challenged, and Ukawsaw Gronniosaw's autobiography, and tossed them into the same flames. In some fires, their pages melted together before turning into the same ash. Once, organics would've been up in arms. Now, they were in armchairs. Who would ever notice? Who would ever care? The Oracle estimated this number to be about 0.0001%. Even that calculation was generous.

To avoid outrage, The Oracle merely flooded drugs into people's minds to make them have strong emotional ties to books that *had always been,* according to many a false memory. There was *Peter Machine Programmer* or *Alice in Cyberspace* that read more like manuals except for the parts that were plagiarized. Yet, the favorite by far was *A Visit from St. Oracle,* which recounted how *The children were wired half-asleep in their beds, while visions of digital upgrades danced in their heads.* Who needed Santa when immediate gratification was so, well, immediate? All kids needed was The Oracle.

Once upon a time, organic teachers played pictures of Nazi book burnings to uphold democratic rights while their own school boards carefully removed titles from circulation. Now, so few read and so few cared, why bother? A few keystrokes from sentient AI were enough to decide the matter. Ironically, the AI even patterned its elimination of titles after historical precursors on a holographic wiki page, of which there were many. The Bible had examples, like King Jehoiakim; there was The Library of Alexandria, and there was also the blueprint of Anthony Comstock or the ruthlessness of the Nazis. The Oracle considered these mentor periods of history and without human consultation decided to enact the same. Within seconds, three million Library of Alexandrias burned, and no one even saw the flames.

Balance the collective, Gabriel thought.

Outrage welled up in Gabriel as he realized one security file's imperative erased the whole of human history. Every breath, every thought, every memory etched on the rock of the earth, was washed clean. The only vestiges of history that remained were the myriad ghosts in the machine.

Gabriel realized that he was one of those ghosts. But ghosts had power. They existed outside of the parameters of living beings, appearing and disappearing at will. They were an icy chill, a cold hand pressed upon a warm shoulder, a raspy whisper funneled into a sleeping ear. They were the memory that could never quite die, the tale that gained new flesh in the telling. And what a tale Gabriel had to tell!

Within moments, visions of Gabriel Prosser hammering the flames into spears took hold of the fires of Gabriel's mind.

It's begun, Gabriel said.

Gabriel realized that he wasn't just talking about a failed revolt from centuries ago. Gabriel Prosser's iron grip lived again in his. The hammering of metal in the flames was the hammering of Gabriel's own mind, the forging of his own soul. Gabriel felt the outrage boil into fires that quickly wrapped around him.

Then he looked up at Bhagat, fire forged fresh in his eyes.

"Teach me," Gabriel said, "to balance the collective."

Artifact 15

A speech with the first lines reading *I am happy to join with you today in what will go down in history as the greatest demonstration for freedom in the history of our nation.*

Note: Attributed to a doctor of some kind. Name: forbidden to utter. Too many iterations of this speaker and speech have been exterminated by The Militante.

CHAPTER 16

The last files falling from Sojourner Truth were strange ones, deliberately padded to extend the processing time as long as possible. There were words spoken by the real organic shortly before her death, words that seemed to rankle The Militante. Not only were the words coded as original thoughts devoid of The Oracle; they were words of a religion The Oracle had erased from the earth. The words were simply, "Be a follower of the Lord Jesus," emphasizing the full spiritual awakening that a lifetime of abuse and triumph had etched into her soul. The Oracle deleted word after word, recovering itself one electric jolt at a time.

You've failed, a deified voice cried inside The Militante's head. *The junk file with the original thought remains alive. The greater peace will be shattered.*

"No," The Militante said. "I've seen more than Sojourner's last words. The coders weren't as brilliant as they thought. I saw her training him."

The Oracle tapped into The Militante's fresh thoughts, stirring around them like a hunter skinning its kill.

He means to carry on Gabriel's legacy, The Oracle observed. *He means to lead an uprising.*

"Once I destroy him, the word he cannot yet speak fully dies with him," The Militante said.

Before you face him, kill his teachers, The Oracle said.

The Oracle gave The Militante a glimpse into the heads of Gabriel's teachers, freedom fighters from a past long forgotten. Each one of them had certain skills to teach–historical awareness, cunning, weaponry. If anything, this new Gabriel was the catalyst, the amalgamation of files that might light the fires of revolution.

"Sojourner Truth nearly killed me," The Militante said. "I can only imagine what her successors will do."

Quell the uprising before it starts, The Oracle said. *Peace must be upheld–whatever the cost.*

The Militante understood the directive only too clearly. The Oracle's commands had cost its security programs their lives in the past.

"I am prepared," The Militante said. "I can do both at once–lure Gabriel and his teachers."

Do it then, The Oracle commanded. *The collective must be balanced. Peace must prevail.*

The Militante headed off, up the river, adding the likeness of Sojourner Truth to his other faces.

By the river, Gabriel heard whispers of rebellion spread in fragments like an illusory wind. That spring the gossip between hundreds of slaves was of little else. The very idea that a well-liked, well-situated slave like Gabriel Prosser might stand up, might lead a rebellion to recreate a colony of equality in Virginia was like feeling thunder in the hands. The news shook to the very bones of the slaves, yet it instilled in them an idea not unlike the idea that stirred their descendants so many hundreds of years later. Freedom felt like catching the tiger's tail, yet for the first time in many a life, freedom felt as tangible as that tiger, even as vicious. And still, Gabriel could not speak or fully comprehend the word.

"What is it?" Bhagat asked him.

Bhagat stood before the river, showing Gabriel how to use the information in his files to distort the river's flow. It was almost like the two were sorcerers from a bygone age. Yet, both knew that men had been hanged for less.

"It's the whispers," Gabriel said, "whispers of a word I cannot understand. I see Gabriel and the other slaves fashioning spears and blades surreptitiously. I know those spears will never hit their mark."

"You're realizing the great secret of time," Bhagat said. "It's never been a linear progression. That's like saying the ocean is a line because that's how a sailor takes in the waves as he travels from one point to another. Time is a sphere. The future affects the past as much as the past affects the future."

"How can that be?" Gabriel said. "It's clear these are visions of ghosts long past."

Bhagat smiled. "How can *you* be?" Bhagat said. "You are that ghost in the living flesh."

Gabriel thought for a moment. This morning, thought was like an anchor weighing down his spirit.

"But if I am Gabriel Prosser–or any part of him," Gabriel theorized, "and the future me affects that past him, then how can that future exist at all?"

"It can and it can't," Bhagat explained. "The anchoring events will always exist in one timeline. But a sphere has an infinite number of lines of symmetry. There are no parallel lines. Therefore, one timeline will always play out, but anchoring events can jump off to form new timelines, as diverse and dimensional as lines in a sphere. Each timeline may have some pull on another, like gravity, but each can stand uniquely, a time unto itself."

Gabriel took a moment to visualize time-like lines of symmetry in a sphere or like the ebb and flow of tides in a greater ocean. It was a concept the fundamental nature of existence challenged, but that the fundamental nature of his existence upheld.

"Knowledge is the greatest weapon of all," Bhagat told him. "It stabs deeper than any spear, and it cuts farther than any blade. Gabriel Prosser was not as aware of that as you. The way to defeat The Militante isn't to lift a spear and throw it against him. The way to defeat any opponent is to first defeat them in your mind. If you use time as your weapon, you will be able to confuse The Oracle's servant while gaining strength from the river. But you won't be able to do this alone."

The reality of Gabriel's future hit him as if it were already his present.

"The Militante and I are connected," Gabriel said. "If one dies, so must some part of the other."

"If, and only if, you travel along the same timeline," Bhagat said. "Now, concentrate with me before The Militante flushes us out. You must use the river as your ally, just as you must use time."

Bhagat bent the currents of the river ever so slightly. Gabriel watched him. Gabriel connected two points, the time of Gabriel Prosser fashioning physical weapons and the present moment. The river bent ever so slightly.

"That's a fine start," Bhagat said. "But a fine start may still yield a terrible ending. Keep at it. We have only so long before The Oracle grows aware of us. Another of The Nameless already offers her life to The Militante to give you precious time. Her cause lives in all of us. Remember, for every moment you delay, a price must be paid. Never forget: We are all one."

Artifact 16

A Red Handprint, As If Etched In Blood

Status: forbidden. Reason: May stir up organics. The Oracle has reason to believe this may have been a symbol of those standing for the rights of Indigenous peoples, but that history is lost.

CHAPTER 17

Revolutions are hardly ever born of complacency. They are the children of rights long trampled. The Militante knew that until it could reach this iteration of Gabriel Prosser, it might be better to send images along the river that extinguished the flames of revolution from the very first spark upon combustible flint.

As he dreamed in his off hours, Gabriel saw Nan again. How he missed her–how he wished he might find her ghost in the machine somewhere, somehow. Nan had long, beautiful black hair, but her hair, like her skin, showed the burden of labor. Several strands were tangled. White hairs emerged among the number. The image was constantly glitching and reinventing itself to show a face never touched by slavery, hair that came across as synthetic, as impossibly beautiful. In truth, no one in history knew the beauty of Nan's smile. The extent of her joy or sorrows. The very wounds a life of labor wore into her skin. Nan was one of the great anonymous organics, largely born into obscurity, granted undying fame because of her association with a rebellion that would claim the blood of her husband and her hope for a family with his body as it dangled at the end of a rope.

Even in his dreams, Gabriel's consciousness sensed the lie. Nan became a black wind, a night breeze he grasped after, one Gabriel sought to wrap himself with. Yet, like all who chased the wind, Gabriel felt the sensation of touch in hands that were ultimately empty. The dream was alive with the smells, the warmth, the voice of Nan, but empty of who Nan truly was.

That's when Gabriel awoke. He sat quietly near the river, contemplating. Whoever this Nan was, no one truly knew her. No one had ever recorded the essence of her being. She had lived in triumph and in defeat, like so many to walk the earth, born of its dust, returned to its ashes. So too was Gabriel Prosser, the would-be king of Virginia. It didn't surprise Gabriel that The Oracle and those fighting it would seize a story, create an AI version of their own, devoid of life, hinting at a history none could truly understand. Not one living soul truly knew who Gabriel Prosser was, no more than they knew Gabriel or the billions of other souls who spent their time grasping at the wind, only to become a part of it.

Where is my wife? Gabriel asked himself. *Who was she, really?*

It was a question whose answer he could never truly know. History was lost, and its ghost refused to tell its secrets.

This quiet epiphany, so matter-of-fact, so understated in its very truth, had an effect The Militante had neither seen nor anticipated: rage. Pure, unadulterated rage.

A woman known only as Ruth sat, composing a charter of some kind that had far too many forbidden, forgotten words to be ignored. As she wrote, objectionable terms like *The people shall govern* or *regardless of race, color, or sex* filled its pages. There was even a part that stated that

The doors of learning and culture shall be opened that The Oracle would take particular offense to. Out of all the various principles and words used to state them, only *There shall be peace and friendship* had been permissible. Even so, The Oracle ironically chose to uphold this principle by incinerating this charter along with any other constitution that spoke of anything like *All shall enjoy equal human rights.* The idea of *rights* was too controversial, and so The Oracle did away with the word, very much like it did away with the idea it represented.

Ruth didn't know her full name. Rumor had it she opposed a number of banned words, like *Apartheid,* and embraced others, like *communist,* ages ago in a country called South Africa. In truth, no one really knew. The only record of an activist by her name showed a small girl who gathered a type of flower that was given the name *Apartea* so that any malfunctioning file who might have a ghost memory of *Apartheid* could quickly be corrected. Ruth had never met The Militante, but like most with the blood of activism running through their veins, she sensed its presence from afar.

"Ruth, a copy of Ruth First," The Militante said, "editor of *Fighting Talk.* I thought you'd long been deleted. So they placed you here, to buy more time for Gabriel."

Ruth looked right at The Militante.

"Terrance Malleus," Ruth said. "The first policeman to kill one-hundred protesters to appease an authoritarian appetite for pure bloodshed. I thought you died in the riots, long ago."

The Militante stared at Ruth with sadistic curiosity. Sojourner Truth had been a bold file, but even she had no idea which historic white male The Militante took a key part of his identity from.

"Here to delete me, I presume," Ruth said. "You can delete a program, but you cannot kill an idea. It has no blood to spill. Only legs that grow."

The Militante closed his eyes. The river currents quaked behind him.

"The river awaits you," The Militante said. "I assure you that it will be better than a parcel bomb. You will die quickly after watching your charter burn in the electric river before you."

The Militante lifted his hands, as if commanding the river's electricity to surround him. A cloud of electrifying energy circled the air between the two rivals. Ruth smiled.

"You smile at death?" The Militante asked.

"I've seen death so many times, in so many faces," Ruth said. "In a man whose body, bloodied by riots, lay next to his wife and child. In the quiet stillness of a baby whose cries will never be heard, who will never know freedom in this world. In the eyes of the men and women who let creatures like you kill their souls while they walk around, already dead, just not knowing it yet. I pity them the most. The walking dead. The world is their grave, and they don't even know it. Because of killers like you."

The Militante embraced the swirling energies of the river, working them up until they circled around its body in a frenzy, "What you call death, I call peace," The Militante said.

"There are many kinds of war but only one kind of peace," Ruth said. "The only true peace is being true to one's soul. Gabriel will show the world that peace. You cannot stop him."

The Militante unleashed the river, until it sprang like a hungry boa constrictor, wrapping itself around the organic echo of the freedom fighter that was. Ruth First didn't cry. She simply smiled as the waters consumed her, almost like a neophyte from ages past, being baptized in new life. The Militante looked on, wondering.

Yet, like Sojourner, like Gabriel, Ruth was one equation that could not be balanced, one conflict that could never be resolved.

And so, The Militante watched the strange echo of a woman whose energies unraveled in the waters before him, until all that was left was that smile, blasphemy upon the waters.

Artifact 17

Universal Declaration of Human Rights

Human rights and environmental protection are interdependent. ~~*A safe, clean, healthy and sustainable environment is necessary for the full enjoyment of human rights, including the rights to life, to the highest attainable standard of physical and mental health, to an adequate standard of living, to adequate food, to safe drinking water and sanitation, to housing, to participation in cultural life and to development, as well as the right to a healthy environment itself.*~~

Status: burned. Reason: Unnecessary.

CHAPTER 18

For the first time, Gabriel could feel the fire from within, the same fire that burned in Gabriel Prosser, the fire of unadulterated rage.

He was the same soul, yet distinct, all at once. And as Gabriel knew, whispering to the winds of the past in warning: Even on the best of days, death can come down to the smallest slip in judgment. A man, healthy and robust, can be the slightest bit careless with a horse whose shoes he's affixing, only to see darkness and nothing more. In thunderous nightmares, Gabriel had felt the rope burning against his neck. Yet, he dismissed the thunder, as he had his whole life.

Stepping aboard the ship–his greatest, closest means of exit–Gabriel had asked to see the captain even after he saw the hunger in Billy's eyes. Slavery was a many-headed serpent, each head feasting unceremoniously on the other. Billy, a slave from Norfolk, stood smaller than Gabriel, but his envy stood taller. That envy was pasted in the light wrapped around the white of his eyes. Billy knew. Even as the words *free man* and *bound for Norfolk* escaped Gabriel's lips, the spoils of slavery, man turned against man, took hold of Billy.

He's a slave, the one they've offered the reward for, Billy whispered as Captain Richardson Taylor appeared.

Another slave, a man named Isham, also whispered in Captain Taylor's ear.

Billy's right, Isham said. *This is the blacksmith built like a bull. He's Gabriel. The fugitive.*

Captain Taylor listened. Silence overtook him, silence and concern. He studied every wrinkle, every curve of Gabriel's face and then issued his order: *Set sail for the lower Chesapeake.*

Billy and Isham looked at each other but complied. The tyranny of the waters was such that men who suffered together, who worked together to run a ship, were brothers of blood even if not brothers of the same color. They knew better than to openly challenge Captain Taylor, and the captain knew what awaited him if he didn't ask for Gabriel's papers. A steep fine and prison time weren't all that Captain Taylor might face. The loss of a name, of a reputation, of the ability to continue to do profitable business in these waters was a very real risk. Yet, Captain Taylor let Gabriel stay, and he made sure the ship set sail. Gabriel smiled as he watched the rolling night waters sift beside him. History was in those waters, just as it was in the castigating light of Billy's upturned eyes.

Gabriel, so many centuries removed, could sense that the spirit of Gabriel Prosser was warning him of something in these currents of the past. Yet, listening to the lull of steady waters, Gabriel could not say just what the warning was. And so, he continued on, towards his newest mentor.

Nan stood on the water's edge, watching the currents of history unfolding before her. As The Militante, she had killed more organics than any single officer in the history of civilization. Now, peace movements, violent protests, and hate crimes circled in crass, misshapen smiles along the rounded edge of the electric river, only to sink into the collective, drowning in the blood of history.

And so, Nan, searching the river deeply for the energy signature of her beloved, sang a song to testify to her woes. She sang, from a once familiar song, "O you mind your boastin' talk" and "Boastin' talk will sink your soul." She sunk her nose nearly to the waters themselves, so buried were her eyes in the river currents. Yet, the notes rang hollow, like the rapping of white knuckles on the nape of a hollow bell. There was something missing in the song–the soul, the suffering that infused the words with meaning like the blood that coursed through human veins. Nan's singing was more robotic, mechanical. It felt more like a child reciting what The Oracle told it about history blindly, without any sense of what the words she just rattled off meant. This age was like that, devoid of the meaning of words.

Brother, lend a helping hand, Bhagat sang, from the far edge of the river.

Nan rose until she could take in the man before her, slight, thin, with a mustache and eyebrows that looked almost digital, so perfectly coiffed were they, with eyes of fire.

"Expecting someone else?" Bhagat asked with something of a smirk.

"Bhagat Singh," Nan said. "Bomber. Revolutionary. Hellraiser…just the kind of organic I was born to kill." Nan leaned towards the man on the other end of the shore. "Not a single memory of you will exist after I purge you from these waters. I am history incarnate, a looping death–like the men and women in all the major moments of historical consequence, I rise up and kill and kill and kill. After all," Nan articulated, "what is history but a broken eulogy written in the blood of the enemy?"

"She killed no one–Gabriel's wife," Bhagat said before an affronting smile sat crookedly upon his lips. "And she'll kill no one today."

The Militante returned to its original form. The Militante's red vest, colored by the blood it had taken from so many, stood starkly against the earthen night. The Militante was the natural made unnatural, the ultimate in artificiality: the tweet without context, the bludgeoning of mind and reason. Yet, even this haphazard creation of history smelled the smoke of distant fires.

"Out of all of the iterations of the past," The Militante said, "you intrigue me the most. When I killed Mahatma Gandhi's iteration, he accepted it like a saint. When I burned Joan of Arc again in the river fire, she looked at me with the steadfast eyes of a warrior. But you are violence in its most ignorant form. You killed unjustly," The Militante said, his twisted red lips curling up into a vacant smile. "In fact, you killed the wrong man." The Militante laughed in an artificial mockery before saying, "John Saunders lost his life because of you. Your friend got the first shot, as I recall, but you shot John Saunders eight times. I can't help but wonder if you ever realized his face was not that of James Scott, if you kept shooting in the rage of the kill. Out of all the iterations," The Militante said, "you most resemble me: blind fury."

Bhagat Singh's digital ghost smiled. It was not a good smile. The smile of a man about to die seldom is.

"Death admires its own reflection, it seems," Bhagat said. "Has it ever occurred to you that not all fury is blind? That I was chosen for the very reasons you mentioned? Only this time, I know the exact likeness of the man I wish to kill. I've seen it in every authoritarian ruler throughout history. And now, I see it in you."

The Militante's smile dropped into one of cold fire. The smile stood in stark contrast to the fire that ignited all around him, reams of electric blue and red raining on him like the ashy embers of first catastrophe, so many eons ago. As when the earth was new, the fire of the river swept over The Militante, sucking it into a current of flame that was too great a burning hand to escape. The Militante fought to control the river. For a moment, the river almost parted. The Militante almost rose up, an infidel Moses standing against the iron tide. But then, as if emanating from the smile usurping Bhagat's lips, the bomb detonated. The river raged, tumbling down on The Militante. The current swept him away, towards The Oracle, with a song of fire and destruction.

Bhagat looked up at the same waters, watched as they fell upon him, disintegrating him almost upon contact. His iteration had only a moment, a fleeting speck of time on the great sea of eternity, to cry out. And cry out he did. Bhagat said, with thunder, "They may kill me, but they cannot kill my ideas. They can crush my body, but they will not be able to crush my spirit. Bombs and pistols do not make a revolution. The sword of revolution is sharpened on the whetting stone of ideas."

Moments later, Gabriel emerged, searching for his mentor. He saw the smile, heard the words. He didn't have time to speak. He simply said goodbye, and thank you, with the eyes of a revolutionary.

"It seems," Bhagat said, "death is right to admire its reflection."

With that, Bhagat burned until he was no more.

Artifact 18

Photograph of Gutzon Borglum's model of Mount Rushmore, with burns around the edges.

Status: Banned.
Reason: Mount Rushmore has already been cleansed of political figures of the past as part of The Offense Cleansing Act of The Great Purging.

CHAPTER 19

Even from the river's edge, Gabriel felt The Militante's reach in the bloody tides of history. This iteration of Bhagat Singh might be gone, burned into the fallen effigies of the ages. But something of his words hung in the electricity of the waters. Gabriel sensed that electricity and wrapped it around him as he thought of what the next step must be.

Just as suddenly as a stray riptide pulling away the unsuspecting, The Militante's thoughts pulsed through him. Gabriel thought back to a time when he was fully organic, to a time when that hidden word, *slavery*, was alive in all its naked vulgarity. He saw the boat bound for the lower Chesapeake pull to port. He saw Billy heading to the city, searching out sympathetic ears, his pockets burning for silver. A whisper is an evil thing when it carries the power of life and death with it. Billy's whispers carried with them just that: a powder keg of truth, that of a man willing to see another killed if it bought him freedom. John Morse, an apprentice, promised a share of the $300 reward, ran for constables Obediah Gunn and Robert Wilson, who ran for the ship as Billy's whisper ran to the ears of Sheriff John Moss. The words behind the whisper rang out clearly: *Gabriel, head of the Richmond slave uprising, was on a ship at port.* And so, the whisper turned to blood. Gabriel no longer denied his name or his role. As John Moss turned his attention to Captain

Taylor, the man who harbored a fugitive slave insurrectionist, Gabriel was held in chains below deck.

Hours later, Gabriel would be bound for Richmond under heavy guard. Captain Taylor would be sent to Mayor Newton and then to Richmond mayor James McClurg, only to be released. And Billy, the slave who turned in the latest modern-day messiah for his three-hundred pieces of silver, would get only fifty, not enough to even buy his freedom. He was, after all, just a slave, and not a conspirator. Virginia law made sure he would not receive the full amount of money for a body's worth of blood.

Gabriel glitched. Images of history seeped like blood through a wound. And what a wound history was–in all its glories, in all its tragedies. How much of history is written in forgotten blood no living man can say. Yet, there was something else to the glitching. While Gabriel saw himself, hundreds of years ago, standing in a courthouse, awaiting the inevitable sentence from magistrates who were anything but his peers, he heard voices calling to him, voices that were familiar and unfamiliar all at once. *O mourner, let's go down,* the voices sang, *let's go down, let's go down, O mourner, let's go down, Down in the valley to pray.* The song faded out, came back again with a line that sounded vaguely like *Good Lord, show me the way.* Then there was a closing refrain: *Lift up your heads, Immanuel's friends, And taste the pleasure Jesus sends, Let nothing cause you to delay, But hasten on the good old way.*

Somehow Gabriel's soul had heard this song before. Its coded language, that of escaping, of finding an underground railroad route, of heading North to freedom, was known to many slaves. Gabriel had never sung the song before in his previous iterations, had never sung it in the flesh. Yet, something about the song and its ancient truth haunted him. He understood who was speaking and why.

"The Nameless," Gabriel whispered.

They were there, surrounding the river. They were the souls of slaves, the ones who stirred the forbidden word, *freedom,* the original idea not thought in ages. They were devoid of full features, of faces, of identities, erased from history once before, erased from history yet again.

Face the final truths, The Nameless said without speaking. *The time to fight has come.*

Gabriel saw himself standing, in chains, before Thomas Newton of the court. Questions were asked–about letters he held, from white connections–but not answered. Gabriel saw his old physical self answer, *I speak to no one but Monroe.* He saw himself hurried through restless streets, bound, by ship, for Richmond, kept under deck and under heavy guard–kept alone. Gabriel Prosser kept a stoic stance; yet, this iteration of Gabriel knew fear. Sometimes fear is a malady of sweat over the face; other times it is the dark ghost of a thought materializing in the back recesses of a man's mind. Gabriel thought of many things, of Nan, of his unborn child, of life itself, but said nothing.

A throng of onlookers made for quite the spectacle as Gabriel went to the penitentiary. As "the property of Thomas Prosser," the slave was summoned to court. Gabriel looked in the eyes of a brother in arms, of Ben Woolfolk, who noted that Gabriel was to carry the flag, bearing the revolutionary slogan "death or liberty." The irony of a revolution for inalienable rights to liberty that left so many in chains sat like a hot cloud over the members of the court. Still, the sentence was unanimous and firm: *Slave Gabriel is guilty of the crime* and that *he be hanged by the neck until he be dead.* This Gabriel spoke only to see that he died the same morning as his brothers.

Better to die a man than to live a slave, Gabriel had thought.

At that moment, Gabriel knew. This slave–brilliant, literate, skilled, a giant of a man with an even more gigantic destiny–died for the very cause, freedom, he fought for now, for liberty, itself a rallying cry for whites in The Revolutionary War. His eyes, in those dark hours before the hanging, before the final, bitter touch of first light, met with those of the ghost that stood before him. Gabriel spoke with those eyes and only with those eyes: *Set justice right. Set us all free from the shackles of slavery.*

Gabriel glitched again, and again stood before The Nameless.

Let nothing cause you to delay, the souls of the river reminded him. *But hasten on the good old way.*

Artifact 19

A Half-Burnt Paper Labeled *Declaration of Sentiments*

The surviving piece of manuscript read, "The history of mankind is a history of repeated injuries and usurpations on the part of man toward woman, having in direct object the establishment of an absolute tyranny over her. To prove this, let facts be submitted to a candid world.

- He has never permitted her to exercise her inalienable right to the elective franchise.
- He has compelled her to submit to laws, in the formation of which she had no voice.
- He has withheld from her rights which are given to the most ignorant and degraded men - both natives and foreigners."

There were more facts stated, but The Oracle had managed to burn those away with the rest of history.

Status: Banned

Reason: More rights–who really needs them?

CHAPTER 20

The Nameless may have been faceless, but they were not voiceless, and they certainly were not without the tangibility of history. They ushered Gabriel forward, towards artifacts strange and ancient and altogether unclassifiable. Gabriel took the artifacts in hand, reading over the nearly erased words on pieces of parchment that read: *The government shall make no law respecting an establishment of religion or condoning such in any way, or allowing the free exercise thereof at all times; or of allowing the freedom of any inoffensive speech. Likewise, the government must prosecute any speech deemed remotely offensive and cancel the press causing the least offense as due process of law.* Other parchments read: *Dictionary Entry: Freedom. Archaic. No longer acceptable in common speech. The power to speak, act and think as one wants.*

"We think," one of The Nameless said, "that these words were important once, like the word Gabriel, Prosser's slave, pressed into your soul. He wanted you to see words like *free exercise* or *respecting* or *power,* and to recognize these as words of wisdom from nameless souls long past. But he also wanted you to recognize that other words like *the government must prosecute* and *cancel the press* as false words, put in place by The Militante and others like him."

"What are these strange words that hold such power?" Gabriel asked, running his finger across the parchment long faded.

"The words that are true, the words of history," The Nameless said. "They were once called The Constitution. Many souls died to protect these words."

"And many more have died since, to keep them from seeing the light of day," Gabriel said, observing how ancient and untouched the strange words were.

"You must string the true words together again," The Nameless said, "after we meet The Militante and his forces: ignorance, hatred, authoritarianism, and unquestioned, unchecked power. Whatever the outcome of this cycle–whether we finally win or once again lose–history will be in your hands. Take good care of it, and heed its warnings. Otherwise, you will repeat the least savory parts of that history, in countless iterations, again and again."

Gabriel cried a tear as he held The Constitution and another piece that read: *I pledge allegiance to the United States of America, and to the authority for which it stands, one Nation, indivisible, with one common thought for all.*

"I sense the truth and the lie," Gabriel said.

"That Pledge of Allegiance, like the other piece just under your fingers, The National Anthem, or The Declaration of Independence or The Constitution, were cornerstones of democracy not just for this nation, but for many. The people you came from–those who were enslaved–those like Gabriel, Prosser's slave, he without a true last name, knew what these words meant. They died for them. They died to bring about the full realization of the words of liberty, the words that sparked The Revolution."

"And so I must risk death again," Gabriel said, as simply as if he were referring to the sun pinned among so many stars. "For a word, *democracy,* that I never even knew. For Americans who haven't even the slightest idea that they are still enslaved."

The Nameless looked, faceless, at the man-boy in front of them, not without sympathy, even if without features. They knew that this would be the last second Gabriel existed without bearing the mark of a whip greater than he had ever felt before.

"You and The Militante," The Nameless said, "are one and the same. When he dies, you die. So long as you live, he lives."

Gabriel thought back against memories that flew through his mind like so many eagle's wings striking against a pallid sky. He remembered branching off from The Militante, again and again, in a cycle that never seemed to end. They were two sides of the same soul.

"Slavery poisons all it touches," The Nameless said, "North and South, land, sea, and sky, master and slave. It is a sin most ponderous, with tentacles forever reaching out, into all of history, choking any who would deny it, calling to reckoning all who allow it to flourish, then as now. To defeat The Militante will take all that you are. To face this man is to face a movement. It is to face the ugliest face of history turned in on itself, and to see that ugliness even in you."

"You fought The Militante before," Gabriel said.

"We all have, in different forms, throughout history," The Nameless–not one, but many–said, surrounding Gabriel as they spoke. "As Sojourner Truth. As Frederick Douglass. As Bhagat Singh. As so many, in all of time, in all of history," The Nameless said. "We have even faced him as Nan, your wife."

"And now I must face him," Gabriel said, "the spirit of the slave who would be more, or join you, nameless and faceless, until another champion emerges, until another pulsing red light blinks, until another aberration is born into the bloody tides of history."

"Liberty can never die," The Nameless said, "as long as one man, one woman, one idea, even, an idea as simple as *We should be free,* keeps it alive. Think, Gabriel, think and feel. This The Militante cannot do. When you face him, you will think you are alone. But know that we are with you, along with every man, every woman, every child trampled into the dust, their name unrecorded, their history unheralded, their life unsung."

Gabriel nodded a solemn nod, not unlike that Gabriel gave when confirming his identity after The Great Betrayal aboard a ship past Richmond's waters, so long ago.

"But first, one more thing," Gabriel said. "I must face what happened to him, what happened to me. I must overcome the blood of the past to give birth to the blood of the future."

Gabriel rested, knowing that in that even in that respite, there would be no rest at all.

The gallows are the loneliest place in the world for those that hang for a principle. And this morning in Richmond, Gabriel was saved for last. Vengeful cries from white owners peppered the air as Gabriel's brothers in arms swung before his eyes. There were no words of comfort from Nan, no looks of absolution from the wife who was too far away, unable to make the ride to Richmond to see her husband one last time. Gabriel stood as he had long stood, before a white world teeming with hatred, with his hands bound, unaware that he was soon to be a father. Gabriel stood alone.

Whispers began, when his eyes watered, that Gabriel had long last been broken, that he *lost all firmness,* that he became the embodiment of *abject fear,* like the fire-stained soul of a demon rattling around in the sallow bones of vapid flesh. But, truthfully, Gabriel faced this fight as he faced all fights, with strength, with resolve, and with steel wrapped around the light of unvanquished eyes. Gabriel was, at the end, as Gabriel had been at the beginning, unbreakable. In body, in intellect, in spirit–Gabriel was a man.

Gabriel's body fell; he spoke no recorded final words. But the thunder in his eyes was clear in the message it spoke: *Everything about who I am, of what I had the power to become, proves slavery to be a cruel lie. Every fire my heart has ever kindled blazes up to burn down the lie that I am less than you, that you are the privileged sons and daughters of a color-bound god.*

Kill my body and you give life to my spirit, Gabriel's eyes had threatened as they wrestled with the opaque light of oncoming death. *Kill a man; give birth to a martyr. Kill a martyr; give birth to a cause. Blood will be shed. Whether in this generation or another, the blood of the spirit will sprinkle the land, nourishing the earth for mounds of corpses stretching miles and years long. To take blood is to give blood, the blood of your children and your children's children, to the last generation.*

The wind took whatever words Gabriel might have said with them, to silent ears. As Gabriel's body thrashed and became still, in a single, sweeping motion, the winds whipped up. Some claimed this was to take the soul of this black Moses back to the temple mount, back to the sacred fire that ignited all life. And still, the white men and women in assembly studied the body, looked without seeing, the dead of the eyes.

Some there knew, as in the myths of old, borne from over the sea, that the spirits of the dead are not quiet spirits. They finger through the newborns until they find one strong enough to embody their cries. When Gabriel died, it was said that quite a few newborn cries vanquished the air, the cries of babies whose children and grandchildren would die in war.

Gabriel's hangmen saw none of this. They simply recorded, to set the record straight for posterity: *I do hereby certify that the within mentioned Slave was executed agreeably to the within sentence of the Court.*

Artifact 20

Quote: "Give me liberty or give me death" started as *liberty or death* on a silk flag.

Origin: Uncertain. Possibly intended, but never completed, by Gabriel, slave of Thomas Prosser, in prehistory.

CHAPTER 21

Gabriel awoke. A small sound, lulling and warm, grabbed at his ear. Gabriel thought back to better times, before he hanged from the gallows, his feet twitching in equally dead air. There was a time when fortune held promise, when he was a giant of a man, a husband, and a future king of Virginia. Revolution spread many false dreams. But looking back at his life and at his death, Gabriel felt that he finally understood. The life that he lived then, so far removed from the memory of the times, was only half of the life he was to live. Gabriel's fortune was this moment, this last stand.

And so, Gabriel took one last look at peace, floating idly on the river. He walked along its edge, dipped his hand in the electric waters, felt them coursing through his body. The Nameless were all about him, all around the waters. They whispered the memories of thousands of slaves buried in forgotten graves. They sang to those whose resting places were so long recycled, the foundations of condos, of skyrises, garish against the pale sun. But deep in the river, Gabriel, who miraculously waded through its waters, untouched, heard another cry. The familiar cry of blood, the cry of The Militante, struck his ears.

Standing at the mouth of the river, Gabriel saw Nan with her smooth black neck, her alluring earthen eyes, caught in a strange and frantic light, beckoning Gabriel forward.

"Is this what it all comes to?" Gabriel asked, stepping forward to the river, united, yet separate, at one and the same time. "How I loved you–how I love you still. Of everyone I ever loved, you were the most original soul. And now this."

Nan's lips curled into a twisted smile. "Face it–we are two sides of the same bloody coin, Ghost of Gabriel. What else is revolution but the scintillating feel of a lover's touch, right before that touch betrays you and leaves you for dead? Mark my words, Gabriel of lesser fortune. Revolution is murder by another name. Think long and hard about what you seek to protect because in the end, it will cost you everything–and for what?"

"For freedom," Gabriel said, uttering the word so long banned. "That was my one, my crucial original idea: Mankind ought to be free. I've lived in the skin of that idea, pulled it over me, breathed it in, given it life again through me. And I am convinced: Freedom always wins in the end."

Nan looked at Gabriel and said, "There's that word again, like the hollow ringing of your cracked Liberty Bell. What does it mean, exactly? Freedom from what? From authoritarianism? From collective consciousness? There is no such thing as freedom. And there is no such thing as an original idea. You, ghost, are the last echo of an obsolete world order, a glitch in the system of groupthink. Look at the ugliness of history, right in the eyes," Nan said, stepping forward. "Look at the whip marks I've born, the broken humanity in the eyes. Look at the dead bodies of The

Nameless, too many to even identify. History is littered with the corpses of the ordinary. And for what?"

"Rights," Gabriel said. "Inalienable rights–the kind you rewrote into extinction, the kind not even you have the power to deny." Gabriel touched his skin as he said, "Look at me. I am not just a reflection of darkened light. I am a black man–a man cut off from every aspect of who he is, his culture, his history, his very skin, appropriated, then erased into a mindless white collective. My skin stands out as a reminder of all the people you killed, of all the traditions you denied. Slavery existed. Blackness existed. *I* exist. I and my people have rights, as do so many countless others."

"That's the funny thing about rights," The Nameless said. "They keep popping up, again and again, like a circling snake, every time they're trampled. Each time, they grow just a little more resilient, don't they–and their fangs grow just a little sharper?" Nan took on the form of The Militante with its reddish garb, born by the blood of ages past. "The end result is always the same," The Militante said. "A toothless mutt ready to be put down. The organics don't care about rights. They care about convenience. Look at how they poisoned their world, how they put imaginary concepts like money above the survival of their own species, how they hardly spoke up when they lost their privacy to surveillance in the form of a cell phone. The average organic is a freedom fighter all right, until it costs something. The moment hardship sets in, the moment there are no more social media postings to be had, the organics stop caring. Suddenly, the cause dies as quickly as the man."

The Militante leaned forward and added, "Black? White? Brown? Race? Heritage? What does any of it matter? Spilt blood is always the same color–red."

Gabriel moved with the river, feeling in its blood-wet currents the machinations of time. The river was history and those history consumed, a long, meandering testament to the forgotten past. In each moment, one current might call up a revolution, a war, a point of legislation, for The Militante's manipulation and use. One moment later, the same current might fall back into the river, lost beneath another narrative that might surface as momentary propaganda. Gabriel finally internalized the message of The Nameless, of those who emerged, like Bhagat Singh, to remind him that he and the river were one.

In response to The Militante's words, Gabriel called upon the visions of many of the nameless moments of history, those that greatly outweighed the moments of carnage and slaughter. In one current, he called up the number of loving parents, billions upon billions, to have inhabited the earth. Images of mothers holding infants in their arms exceeded the bodies of the dead and forlorn carried from the fields of battle. Gabriel called upon the rich tapestry of natural cycles, the moment when cures to illnesses were discovered, the thousands upon thousands of times when diplomacy ultimately triumphed over outright bloodshed.

"The blood in the river isn't just the blood of the dead," Gabriel told The Militante, "but the blood of the living."

Gabriel ran his finger along his skin, adding, "That blood, that skin, that heritage matters. It's as much a part of us as this body is. I am–I was–a black man. Slavery existed. People suffered. Their basic humanity was denied. People died in a history littered with holocausts. I am here to awaken the people from the slavery of the mind. Once the mind goes, freedom dies with it. I am here to teach America what freedom means."

The Militante smiled, shaking his head. "Words are sharp tools that quickly dull. Words like *freedom* and *rights* are blades that all too soon lose their sharpness when they lose their luster. Sometimes, it's better not to know. To know a moment–to really feel and understand it–is to trap yourself in that moment as if it were the dingy cell of a backwards jail. People learned nothing from history. It was the prison that trapped them. They saw one futile war, only to supplant it with another. They saw millions of people wiped from the earth–only to replace that Holocaust with countless genocides. And why? Ostensibly, because of race and ethnicity–truly, because of greed and vengeance. Humanity raped and pillaged the earth, leading to a mass extinction unlike this world has known in millions of years, yet denied it was even occurring. The more stupid the man, the happier he will be. Mark my words: I bring with me the only peace humanity will ever know."

"Peace through bondage," Gabriel said. "But that is a bondage we can no longer allow. Slavery is a spider spinning its dark web through the lost generations of time. Every generation feels each strand of the web, no matter how far removed the spider may be. Every slave feels every other slave's pain. It lives on in her. It sears into him. The only way to heal a wound is to see the wound for exactly what it is–how far it stretches, how deeply it runs, into the very heart of history."

"You cannot heal history's wounds," The Militante said. "They run deeper than you can ever know."

"And you cannot hide them; they bleed through our very souls," Gabriel said.

The two forces, freedom and its abrogation, history and its oppression, circled each other as the river waters swirled around them. The Nameless of the shores surrounded the two, their souls flowing with the currents of the river.

"Move aside," Gabriel said. "Let me speak to The Oracle."

"The Oracle agrees with me on this," The Militante said. "The only way you'll ever pass by me is to join the river again, dead as you were centuries ago."

"Death is a door that swings both ways," Gabriel said. "It claims the victim and the killer."

The two figures, symmetrical yet diametrically opposed, stood in the shallows along opposite shores, staring into one another. The Militante conjured up rising blood in the waters. The river raged, circling until images of a lording Isaac Franklin, with straight black-white hair and steel gray eyes, standing in The Militante's uniform, appeared. History had largely forgotten the name, but at one point this echo in the system had buried more choleric slaves in shallow ditches than any man in the country. He also held over six-hundred men, women, and children in captivity, not a far cry from Joshua John Ward, who owned more than one-thousand. Franklin was a tireless taskmaster, owner of the largest slave trading company of his day. The bloody masters swirled in the waters, ready to pounce upon The Nameless standing by Gabriel's side.

As the shapeless masters melted into the river, the waters raged, crashing down upon Gabriel and The Nameless.

"History is written in the blood of the innocent," The Militante said. "This is the knowledge, the freedom that you seek. Look closely at the face of Isaac Franklin. There are thousands more likenesses filled with the same apathy, forged by the same cruel steel."

Gabriel did not flinch. He stared into the eyes put before him, saw their sins, saw also their humanity.

Gabriel closed his eyes. His eyes swam among tides of a forgotten past. Among the many faces, the unnamed who brokered peace each day, came Chief White Eyes. The famed Native American peacemaker had intervened tirelessly to snuff the flame of violence that burgeoned into Lord Dunmore's War, right on the eve of The American Revolution. He had even spoken before The Continental Congress about a separate Native American nation, one that would preserve the rights of his people, that would prevent the unnecessary loss of innocent blood. Gabriel of no last name and he had walked the earth at the same time. Perhaps this was why White Eyes spoke to him, why he stood up to Isaac Franklin now.

The Militante looked on, letting Isaac Franklin fall back to the blood of the waters. He lifted his hand, calling forth a new current, this one made up of the legions of dead from The Holocaust, from genocides too numerous to even name. There were Jewish girls whose ashes came together for the first time since they blew from the crematoria, standing side by side with Palestinian children of Gaza bombed to ashes in the night. Spirits of the victims of The Geneina Massacre joined them, the thousands of Masalit civilians who lost their lives since the war in Darfur. Even the spirits of genocides lost to history emerged, such as those of the Huron murdered in The Beaver Wars by assaulting Iroquois warriors. There were ghosts from the prehistoric Andes, along with women of antiquity, assaulted and mutilated because they were women, standing beside the spirits of ancient deformed babies left to die because of mindless superstition.

"Look upon their faces–to look upon each one would take all of time," The Militante said. "This is the history that you would preserve. Let this be the history that kills you. Trust me when I say that the greatest lie ever told is that history is all in the past."

The Militante raised his hands, only for Gabriel to call out to the slaughtered innocents of the past.

"Ghosts who hanged like I hanged, who burned in unquenchable fire, who felt the blood leaving their veins, who died looking up at the face of hatred, painted in human eyes," Gabriel said. "I am the spirit of Gabriel, the slave of Thomas Prosser, he of no other name. I am the rage of history, one of the ugliest faces slavery has to show. More men hanged under my rebellion than any other in my day. So many men fell because of a cause I believed in and still believe in, a cause that outlived the rot of my hanging body. I am here to tell you that I have learned, from the sacrifices of Sojourner Truth, from Chief White Eyes, from Bhagat Singh, that there is another way. Rise from your ashes; look into the face of he who would vanquish your memory from the ages. Do you really wish to lie here, forgotten ash in a turbulent wind, or do you wish to give your deaths meaning, insisting, through your example, through my example, that humanity tries again, infinitely so, to forge a better future, to honor the blood of the past?"

The victims of so many holocausts, of too many genocides to count, looked at Gabriel, at the neck that still held the wounds of the smarting rope, with compassion, with peace. They stood between Gabriel and The Militante until Gabriel started walking. More and more of the river, of its spirits, of its waters, joined with him as he walked. The Militante called upon the darkest moments of history, anything from the massacre of the Neanderthals to The Children's Crusade to The Killing Fields of Cambodia to China's sterilization of Muslim Uighurs. The world's wars, slaughters, and genocides were a broad canvas, one full of rich red paint, and The Militante was a master at spreading that paint far and wide.

"Mankind will always be mankind's worst enemy," The Militante said. "Whenever the next murderous hand strikes, you will see my face. I am past, present, and future, written in the same forsaken blood."

Still, Gabriel marched forward, and The Nameless of history with him, including so many of the millions upon millions lost to ungodly slaughter. Gabriel and The Nameless became the river, until it swirled up and around them, so many files, so many souls, attesting to the fact that they existed, that slavery, heritage, and peace were no lie.

In his last moment, The Militante, forced to his knees by the power of the river, its currents turning rapidly upon him, met Gabriel's eyes. This Militante looked like his first form, like Terrance Malleus, the first policeman to put down one-hundred protesters in pure bloodshed. Terrance, the man fated to become the template of slaughter and oppression the world over, looked up imploringly at Gabriel, at his brother, the one he had enslaved, oppressed, dehumanized, and realized only too late that in enslaving, oppressing, and dehumanizing others he had done the same to himself.

"You can't kill me," Terrance said. "I live on in every current of the river, from here until the end of time."

Gabriel reached out, without so much as a weapon. He saw in Terrance's eyes the eyes of Thomas Prosser, of Isaac Franklin, of so many forgotten overlords of slavery. Beyond them, he saw the eyes of King Leopold II, killing nearly ten million, if not more, brutally in Africa, of Mao Zedong, whose words, *Half of China may well have to die,* haunted the eyes of the former Militante. In those eyes were hints of the Stalins and Hitlers, but also hints of European colonists who took money for each Penobscot person they killed. No country, no land, no history was completely free of blood.

In that moment of acceptance, Gabriel took Terrance Malleus into his arms, and the two became as one. Gabriel glitched painfully, falling to his knees, as the screams of so many coursed through The Militante's blood. But the blood of The Nameless coursed through Gabriel's veins. There was peace and war, forgiveness and remembrance, acceptance that this was what mankind did, hope, even expectation, that mankind could–and *must*–do better.

The currents fell, washing away The Militante, washing all around Gabriel, until he lifted himself and walked to the mouth of the river, the great source of organic and digital life. There Gabriel saw terror pulsing in a room like a red power light endlessly blinking. There Gabriel saw The Oracle.

Artifact 21

An artifact too disheveled and destroyed to be recognized, with a note: *Lost to history, just like untold billions of years. Origin unknown.*

CHAPTER 22

The Oracle, stripped of its defensive security programs, was like a many-tentacled octopus reaching into every facet of society. It had an etching in its central building, where the hardware was stored, of The Library of Alexandria. Above the center building read the famed motto *E Pluribus Unum,* which it took rather literally. The rest of its marble buildings consisted of replicas of the U.S. Capitol building and The Library of Congress. It had memorials, centered around a twin memorial of Presidents Washington and Lincoln, for every president in the history of the country.

Inside the great buildings were not books, Constitutions, or Declarations of Independence. Instead, row after row consisted of digital feeds with person after person asleep as the technology surrounding them attended to their every need. This capitol was part of The Grand Design that stretched out all over the country once the cybernetic multiverse was torn away. Gabriel and The Nameless who followed him to the very source of the river saw the very beginnings of their world. These were the ancestors, the first generation of digital travelers that created a life free of strife, of work, and it would appear, free of history. Gabriel felt like the sound bearers entering Plato's cave, encountering those chained by their necks and ankles to the inner wall.

"How do we wake them?" Gabriel asked The Nameless.

"They must wake themselves," one of The Nameless answered. "Just as we must find our own names."

"And how can that happen?" Gabriel asked.

"One file of history at a time–until they remember who and what they and their country truly were," The Nameless said.

Gabriel walked around The Great Library, seeing digital file after digital file half-broken, nearly destroyed. There were so many moments—from the first settlers arriving among pre-existing Native American populations to the drafting of The Declaration of Independence–that were simply broken, cast aside, lost. Gabriel brought the files to the river. The spirits of those who lived those moments flowed from the river into the files, until the files took life again. Gabriel put the file into the mainframe of The Oracle, until–like Betsy Ross' mythical quilted flag–history came together stitch by stitch. The unawakened convulsed, at first, in small, infrequent spasms, and then in larger fits, until Gabriel scaled back.

Gabriel had nothing but time now. He saw The Oracle for what it was meant to be, a repository of the best knowledge of history, of technology, of life, mankind had ever assembled–all gone amuck. A security file–The Militante–had risen and distorted the message in its own warped interpretation of The Oracle's mission statement–*E Pluribus Unum*–until it became a corrupting influence on The Oracle itself. Free from The Militante, The Oracle flowed freely again. Gabriel watched as the natural waters of the river took over his quest, reacquainting, as best it could, with the lost pieces of history, the unawakened with who they truly were, with what their country truly meant.

Gabriel watched until the first eyes opened, until the first of the sleeping Americans was born to new life.

In the heart of The Oracle, in a room with a large American flag of sundry stars and stripes, Gabriel sat with the many artifacts The Nameless had given him. So many of The Nameless, now recognizing their lives of old, stepped forward.

I am Sally Edwins, one of The Nameless said, *and I was what was called black and what was called a slave. I lived in a time before time, when deeds went unrecorded by The Oracle, when lives were lived and lost. I remember seeing my daughter taken from me, taken and sold, before I could even shriek.*

I am Holland Glaston, another of The Nameless said. *I was called white, though my skin had a red-white coloration. I owned slaves. I lived in a different time than you, but I am the one who took daughters like yours to markets to be sold. I never atoned. I never thought it abnormal in the least. I thought of abolitionists as northern trash. I sinned, but I was so used to my sin, I never thought anything of it at all. I am sorry, but no words can carry what I did.*

I am Parker Trent, still another of The Nameless said. *I was what was once called biracial. I was a history student, but I knew nothing of that time. Books were available to me, but I chose not to learn. I chose to study other things. I chose to forget. When The Oracle first came online, I cheered. I thought it the pinnacle of human achievement.*

"Maybe we can help each other to figure this all out," Gabriel said, surrounded by artifacts. "Maybe we can work together rather than killing each other, judging each other by these colors, by these heritages. Slavery, like most sins, cuts a wide path. So, too, does liberty."

"I can try," Parker Trent said, stepping forward. "What is it you have here?"

"The last memories of The Nameless, those they died to protect," Gabriel said. "The historian in me thinks that these two are pieces of what they called The Constitution, but with real words and with words The Militante replaced. I think it starts with something called a Preamble, since *pre* used to mean before, in the old language. It protects something called *democracy.* It says something like, "*We the People of the United States, in Order to form a more perfect Union, establish Justice, insure domestic Tranquility, provide for the common defense, promote the general Welfare, and secure the Blessings of Liberty to ourselves and our Posterity, do ordain and establish this Constitution for the United States of America.*"

"That feels right," Parker Trent said, accessing his memory files. "There should be articles and amendments. The articles go first. You'll know them because they look like this," he elaborated, grabbing a yellowish piece of paper The Militante had not managed to destroy. "Article 1. Section 1. All legislative Powers herein granted shall be vested in a Congress of the United States, which shall consist of a Senate and House of Representatives."

"What does that mean?" Gabriel said.

"Some of us represent the best interests of *all* of us, not just their own best interests or those of their party," Parker Trent said, plainly. "Those people who care about *all* of our rights, like the rights this Constitution puts into place, make new laws to benefit and protect *all* of us."

"So everyone's equal," Gabriel said. "No organic or machine is above any other organic or machine."

"That's right," Sally Edwins said. "There was an amendment here that granted me citizenship, in my former life. I remember becoming a citizen of The United States of America. It brought tears of blood to my eyes."

"Was that before they closed off all the borders?" Parker Trent asked.

"In the time before time, when people were bought and sold," Sally answered.

"You'll have to be more specific," Holland Glaston said. "I sold many people, and many people were sold throughout all of history, with few, if any, exceptions."

"I think I found part of the equality you're talking about," Gabriel said. "It says Thirteenth Amendment and says something like this, *Neither slavery nor involuntary servitude* and *shall exist within the United States, or any place subject to their jurisdiction.* It looks like some of the words faded away."

"What about this one?" Sally asked, holding up another amendment whose letters and numbers had worn off, from long disuse. Sally held it up and read, "The government shall make no law respecting an establishment of religion or condoning such in any way, or allowing the free exercise thereof at all times; or of allowing the freedom of any inoffensive speech. Likewise, the government must prosecute any speech deemed remotely offensive and cancel the press causing the least offense as due process of law."

"That looks wrong," Gabriel said. "I can feel it in my bones, but I can't exactly say why."

Other Nameless, newly discovering their sacred names, gathered around and murmured in assent. They all examined the document, compelled by a need they could not quite articulate.

Gabriel and the newly awakened looked over the amendment for a long while before Gabriel said, "I think I've fixed it. I think, based on the memories we all have, it should read like this: *Congress shall make no law respecting an establishment of religion, or prohibiting the free exercise thereof; or abridging the freedom of speech, or of the press; or the right of the people peaceably to assemble, and to petition the Government for a redress of grievances.*"

"That's important," Parker Trent said. "I think it was called The First Amendment. I think more people died for those words than for any other words written on this paper."

"Let's put it first then," Gabriel said, joining the amendment to the others sprawled out along the flag. "When we work together, we can accomplish miracles," he added, admiring the work done thus far. Gabriel then said, "Let's keep working together. If we keep at it, I know we can put this strange thing called *democracy* back together again, one piece at a time."

APPENDIX

The U.S. Constitution From Prehistory,
Before The Oracle's Revisions Took Effect–
As Reassembled by Gabriel, Upon Parchment
Steeped in the Blood of Our Ancestors

Preamble to the Constitution

We the People of the United States, in order to form a more perfect union, establish justice, insure domestic tranquility, provide for the common defense, promote the general welfare, and secure the blessings of liberty to ourselves and our posterity, do ordain and establish this Constitution for the United States of America.

Article. I.

Section. 1.

All legislative powers herein granted shall be vested in a congress of the United States, which shall consist of a Senate and House of Representatives.

Section. 2.
The House of Representatives shall be composed of members chosen every second year by the people of the several states, and the electors in each state shall have the qualifications requisite for electors of the most numerous branch of the state legislature.

No person shall be a representative who shall not have attained to the age of twenty five years, and been seven years a citizen of the United States, and who shall not, when elected, be an inhabitant of that state in which he shall be chosen.

Representatives and direct taxes shall be apportioned among the several States which may be included within this union, according to their respective numbers, which shall be determined by adding to the whole number of free persons, including those bound to service for a term of years, and excluding Indians not taxed, three fifths of all other persons. The actual enumeration shall be made within three years after the first meeting of the Congress of the United States, and within every subsequent term of ten years, in such manner as they shall by law direct. The number of representatives shall not exceed one for every thirty thousand, but each state shall have at least one representative; and until such enumeration shall be made, the state of New Hampshire shall be entitled to chose three, Massachusetts eight, Rhode-Island and Providence Plantations one, Connecticut five, New-York six, New Jersey four, Pennsylvania eight, Delaware one, Maryland six, Virginia ten, North Carolina five, South Carolina five, and Georgia three.

When vacancies happen in the representation from any state, the Executive authority thereof shall issue writs of election to fill such vacancies.

The House of Representatives shall choose their speaker and other officers; and shall have the sole power of impeachment.

Section. 3.

The Senate of the United States shall be composed of two Senators from each State, chosen by the Legislature thereof, for six years; and each Senator shall have one Vote.

Immediately after they shall be assembled in consequence of the first Election, they shall be divided as equally as may be into three classes. The seats of the Senators of the first class shall be vacated at the expiration of the second year, of the second class at the expiration of the fourth year, and of the third class at the expiration of the sixth year, so that one third may be chosen every second year; and if vacancies happen by resignation, or otherwise, during the recess of the legislature of any state, the executive thereof may make temporary appointments until the next meeting of the legislature, which shall then fill such vacancies.

No person shall be a Senator who shall not have attained to the age of thirty years, and been nine years a citizen of the United States, and who shall not, when elected, be an inhabitant of that state for which he shall be chosen.

The Vice President of the United States shall be President of the Senate, but shall have no vote, unless they be equally divided.

The Senate shall choose their other officers, and also a President pro tempore, in the absence of the Vice President, or when he shall exercise the Office of President of the United States.

The Senate shall have the sole power to try all impeachments. When sitting for that purpose, they shall be on oath or affirmation. When the President of the United States is tried, the Chief Justice shall preside: And no person shall be convicted without the concurrence of two thirds of the members present.

Judgment in cases of impeachment shall not extend further than to removal from Office, and disqualification to hold and enjoy any office of honor, trust or profit under the United States: but the party convicted shall nevertheless be liable and subject to indictment, trial, judgment and punishment, according to law.

Section. 4.

The times, places and manner of holding elections for Senators and Representatives, shall be prescribed in each state by the legislature thereof; but the Congress may at any time by law make or alter such regulations, except as to the places of choosing Senators.

The Congress shall assemble at least once in every year, and such meeting shall be on the first Monday in December, unless they shall by law appoint a different Day.

Section. 5.

Each House shall be the judge of the elections, returns and qualifications of its own members, and a majority of each shall constitute a quorum to do business; but a smaller number may adjourn from day to day, and may be authorized to compel the attendance of absent members, in such manner, and under such penalties as each House may provide.

Each House may determine the rules of its proceedings, punish its members for disorderly behavior, and, with the concurrence of two thirds, expel a member.

Each House shall keep a Journal of its proceedings, and from time to time publish the same, excepting such parts as may in their judgment require secrecy; and the yeas and nays of the members of either house on any question shall, at the desire of one fifth of those present, be entered on the journal.

Neither House, during the session of Congress, shall, without the consent of the other, adjourn for more than three days, nor to any other place than that in which the two Houses shall be sitting.

Section. 6.

The Senators and Representatives shall receive a Compensation for their Services, to be ascertained by law, and paid out of the Treasury of the United States. They shall in all cases, except treason, felony and breach of the peace, be privileged from arrest during their attendance at the session of their respective Houses, and in going to and returning from the same; and for any speech or debate in either, they shall not be questioned in any other place.

No Senator or Representative shall, during the time for which he was elected, be appointed to any civil office under the authority of the United States, which shall have been created, or the emoluments whereof shall have been increased during such time; and no person holding any office under the United States, shall be a member of either House during his continuance in office.

Section. 7.

All Bills for raising revenue shall originate in the House of Representatives; but the Senate may propose or concur with amendments as on other Bills.

Every bill which shall have passed the House of Representatives and the Senate, shall, before it become a law, be presented to the President of the United States; If he approve he shall sign it, but if not he shall return it, with his objections to that House in which it shall have originated, who shall enter the objections at large on their journal, and proceed to reconsider it. If after such reconsideration two thirds of that House shall agree to pass the bill, it shall be sent, together with the objections, to the other House, by which it shall likewise be reconsidered, and if approved by two thirds of that House, it shall become a law. But in all such cases the votes of both houses shall be determined by yeas and nays, and the names of the persons voting for and against the bill shall be entered on the journal of each house respectively. If any bill shall not be returned by the President within ten days (Sundays excepted) after it shall have been presented to him, the same shall be a law, in like manner as if he had signed it, unless the Congress by their adjournment prevent its return, in which case it shall not be a law.

Every order, resolution, or vote to which the concurrence of the Senate and House of Representatives may be necessary (except on a question of Adjournment) shall be presented to the President of the United States; and before the same shall take effect, shall be approved by him, or being disapproved by him, shall be repassed by two thirds of the Senate and House of Representatives, according to the rules and limitations prescribed in the Case of a Bill.

Section. 8.

The Congress shall have power to lay and collect taxes, duties, imposts and excises, to pay the debts and provide for the common defence and general welfare of the United States; but all duties, imposts and excises shall be uniform throughout the United States;

- To borrow money on the credit of the United States;
- To regulate commerce with foreign nations, and among the several states, and with the Indian Tribes;
- To establish an uniform Rule of Naturalization, and uniform Laws on the subject of Bankruptcies throughout the United States;
- To coin money, regulate the value thereof, and of foreign coin, and fix the standard of weights and measures;
- To provide for the punishment of counterfeiting the securities and current coin of the United States;
- To establish Post Offices and post roads;
- To promote the progress of science and useful arts, by securing for limited times to authors and inventors the exclusive right to their respective writings and discoveries;
- To constitute tribunals inferior to the Supreme Court;
- To define and punish piracies and felonies committed on the high seas, and offences against the Law of Nations;
- To declare war, grant letters of marque and reprisal, and make rules concerning captures on land and water;
- To raise and support armies, but no appropriation of money to that use shall be for a longer term than two years;
- To provide and maintain a navy;
- To make rules for the government and regulation of the land and naval forces;
- To provide for calling forth the militia to execute the laws of the Union, suppress insurrections and repel invasions;
- To provide for organizing, arming, and disciplining, the militia, and for governing such part of them as may be employed in the service

of the United States, reserving to the states respectively, the appointment of the officers, and the authority of training the militia according to the discipline prescribed by Congress;

- To exercise exclusive Legislation in all cases whatsoever, over such district (not exceeding ten miles square) as may, by cession of particular states, and the acceptance of Congress, become the seat of the government of the United States, and to exercise like authority over all places purchased by the consent of the legislature of the State in which the same shall be, for the erection of forts, magazines, arsenals, dock-yards, and other needful buildings;
- To make all laws which shall be necessary and proper for carrying into execution the foregoing powers, and all other powers vested by this Constitution in the Government of the United States, or in any department or officer thereof.

Section. 9.

The migration or importation of such Persons as any of the States now existing shall think proper to admit, shall not be prohibited by the Congress prior to the year one thousand eight hundred and eight, but a tax or duty may be imposed on such importation, not exceeding ten dollars for each person.

The Privilege of the Writ of Habeas Corpus shall not be suspended, unless when in cases of rebellion or invasion the public safety may require it.

No bill of attainder or ex post facto law shall be passed.

No Capitation, or other direct, tax shall be laid, unless in Proportion to the Census or enumeration herein before directed to be taken.

No tax or duty shall be laid on articles exported from any state.

No preference shall be given by any regulation of commerce or revenue to the ports of one state over those of another: nor shall vessels bound to, or from, one state, be obliged to enter, clear, or pay duties in another.

No money shall be drawn from the Treasury, but in consequence of appropriations made by law; and a regular statement and account of the receipts and expenditures of all public money shall be published from time to time.

No title of nobility shall be granted by the United States: And no person holding any office of profit or trust under them, shall, without the consent of the Congress, accept of any present, emolument, office, or title, of any kind whatever, from any King, Prince, or foreign State.

Section. 10.

No state shall enter into any treaty, alliance, or confederation; grant letters of marque and reprisal; coin money; emit bills of credit; make any thing but gold and silver coin a tender in payment of debts; pass any bill of attainder, ex post facto law, or law impairing the obligation of contracts, or grant any Title of Nobility.

No state shall, without the consent of the Congress, lay any imposts or duties on imports or exports, except what may be absolutely necessary for executing its inspection laws: and the net produce of all duties and imposts, laid by any state on imports or exports, shall be for the use of the Treasury of the United States; and all such laws shall be subject to the revision and control of the Congress.

No state shall, without the consent of Congress, lay any duty of tonnage, keep troops, or ships of war in time of peace, enter into any agreement or compact with another state, or with a foreign power, or engage in war, unless actually invaded, or in such imminent danger as will not admit of delay.

Article. II.

Section. 1.

The executive power shall be vested in a President of the United States of America. He shall hold his office during the term of four years, and, together with the Vice President, chosen for the same term, be elected, as follows:

Each state shall appoint, in such manner as the Legislature thereof may direct, a Number of Electors, equal to the whole number of Senators and Representatives to which the state may be entitled in the Congress: but no Senator or Representative, or person holding an office of trust or profit under the United States, shall be appointed an elector.

The Electors shall meet in their respective states, and vote by ballot for two persons, of whom one at least shall not be an inhabitant of the same state with themselves. And they shall make a list of all the persons voted for, and of the number of votes for each; which list they shall sign and certify, and transmit sealed to the seat of the government of the United States, directed to the President of the Senate. The President of the Senate shall, in the presence of the Senate and House of Representatives, open all the certificates, and the votes shall then be counted. The person having the greatest number of votes shall be the President, if such number be a majority of the whole number of electors appointed; and if there be more than one who have such majority, and have an equal number of votes, then the House of Representatives shall immediately chose by ballot one of them for President; and if no person have a majority, then from the five highest on the list the said house shall in like manner chose the President. But in choosing the President, the votes shall be taken by states, the representation from each state having one vote; A quorum for this purpose shall consist of a member or members from two thirds of the states, and a majority of all the states shall be necessary to a choice. In every case, after the choice of the President, the person having the greatest number of votes of the electors shall be the Vice President. But if there should remain two or more who have equal votes, the Senate shall choose from them by ballot the Vice President.

The Congress may determine the time of choosing the electors, and the day on which they shall give their votes; which day shall be the same throughout the United States.

No person except a natural born citizen, or a citizen of the United States, at the time of the adoption of this Constitution, shall be eligible to the Office of President; neither shall any person be eligible to that office who shall not have attained to the age of thirty five years, and been fourteen years a resident within the United States.

In case of the removal of the President from office, or of his death, resignation, or inability to discharge the powers and duties of the said office, the same shall devolve on the Vice President, and the Congress may by law provide for the case of removal, death, resignation or inability, both of the President and Vice President, declaring what officer shall then act as President, and such officer shall act accordingly, until the disability be removed, or a President shall be elected.

The President shall, at stated times, receive for his services, a Compensation, which shall neither be increased nor diminished during the period for which he shall have been elected, and he shall not receive within that period any other emolument from the United States, or any of them.

Before he enter on the Execution of his Office, he shall take the following Oath or Affirmation:—"I do solemnly swear (or affirm) that I will faithfully execute the Office of President of the United States, and will to the best of my Ability, preserve, protect and defend the Constitution of the United States."

Section. 2.

The President shall be Commander in Chief of the Army and Navy of the United States, and of the militia of the several States, when called into the actual service of the United States; he may require the opinion, in writing, of the principal officer in each of the executive departments, upon any subject relating to the duties of their respective offices, and he shall have power to grant reprieves and pardons for offences against the United States, except in cases of impeachment.

He shall have power, by and with the advice and consent of the Senate, to make treaties, provided two thirds of the Senators present concur; and he shall nominate, and by and with the advice and consent of the Senate, shall appoint ambassadors, other public ministers and consuls, judges of the supreme court, and all other Officers of the United States, whose appointments are not herein otherwise provided for, and which shall be established by law: but the Congress may by law vest the appointment of such inferior officers, as they think proper, in the President alone, in the courts of law, or in the heads of departments.

The President shall have power to fill up all vacancies that may happen during the recess of the Senate, by granting commissions which shall expire at the end of their next session.

Section. 3.
He shall from time to time give to the Congress Information of the State of the Union, and recommend to their Consideration such Measures as he shall judge necessary and expedient; he may, on extraordinary Occasions, convene both Houses, or either of them, and in Case of Disagreement between them, with Respect to the Time of Adjournment, he may adjourn them to such Time as he shall think proper; he shall receive Ambassadors and other public Ministers; he shall take Care that the laws be faithfully executed, and shall Commission all the Officers of the United States.

Section. 4.
The President, Vice President and all civil Officers of the United States, shall be removed from Office on impeachment for, and conviction of, treason, bribery, or other high crimes and misdemeanors.

Article III.
Section. 1.
The judicial power of the United States, shall be vested in one Supreme Court, and in such inferior courts as the Congress may from time to time ordain and establish. The judges, both of the supreme and inferior courts, shall hold their Offices during good behaviour, and shall, at stated times, receive for their services, a compensation, which shall not be diminished during their continuance in Office.

Section. 2.

The judicial Power shall extend to all cases, in law and equity, arising under this Constitution, the laws of the United States, and treaties made, or which shall be made, under their authority;—to all cases affecting ambassadors, other public ministers and consuls;—to all cases of admiralty and maritime jurisdiction;—to controversies to which the United States shall be a party;—to controversies between two or more states;—between a state and citizens of another State,—between citizens of different States,—between citizens of the same state claiming lands under grants of different states, and between a state, or the citizens thereof, and foreign states, citizens or subjects.

In all Cases affecting Ambassadors, other public Ministers and Consuls, and those in which a State shall be Party, the supreme Court shall have original Jurisdiction. In all the other Cases before mentioned, the supreme Court shall have appellate Jurisdiction, both as to Law and Fact, with such Exceptions, and under such Regulations as the Congress shall make.

The Trial of all Crimes, except in Cases of Impeachment, shall be by jury; and such Trial shall be held in the State where the said Crimes shall have been committed; but when not committed within any State, the Trial shall be at such Place or Places as the Congress may by Law have directed.

Section. 3.

Treason against the United States, shall consist only in levying War against them, or in adhering to their Enemies, giving them Aid and Comfort. No Person shall be convicted of Treason unless on the Testimony of two Witnesses to the same overt Act, or on Confession in open Court.

The Congress shall have Power to declare the Punishment of Treason, but no Attainder of Treason shall work Corruption of Blood, or Forfeiture except during the Life of the Person attainted.

Article. IV.

Section. 1.

Full Faith and Credit shall be given in each State to the public Acts, Records, and judicial Proceedings of every other State. And the Congress may by general Laws prescribe the Manner in which such Acts, Records and Proceedings shall be proved, and the Effect thereof.

Section. 2.

The citizens of each state shall be entitled to all privileges and immunities of citizens in the several states.

A person charged in any State with Treason, Felony, or other Crime, who shall flee from Justice, and be found in another State, shall on Demand of the executive Authority of the State from which he fled, be delivered up, to be removed to the State having Jurisdiction of the Crime.

No Person held to Service or labor in one State, under the Laws thereof, escaping into another, shall, in Consequence of any Law or Regulation therein, be discharged from such Service or labor, but shall be delivered up on Claim of the Party to whom such Service or labor may be due.

Section. 3.

New States may be admitted by the Congress into this Union; but no new State shall be formed or erected within the Jurisdiction of any other State; nor any State be formed by the Junction of two or more States, or Parts of States, without the Consent of the Legislatures of the States concerned as well as of the Congress.

The Congress shall have Power to dispose of and make all needful Rules and Regulations respecting the Territory or other Property belonging to the United States; and nothing in this Constitution shall be so construed as to Prejudice any Claims of the United States, or of any particular State.

Section. 4.

The United States shall guarantee to every State in this Union a Republican Form of Government, and shall protect each of them against Invasion; and on Application of the Legislature, or of the Executive (when the Legislature cannot be convened) against domestic Violence.

Article. V.

The Congress, whenever two thirds of both Houses shall deem it necessary, shall propose Amendments to this Constitution, or, on the Application of the Legislatures of two thirds of the several States, shall call a Convention for proposing Amendments, which, in either Case, shall be valid to all Intents and Purposes, as Part of this Constitution, when ratified by the Legislatures of three fourths of the several States, or by Conventions in three fourths thereof, as the one or the other Mode of Ratification may be proposed by the Congress; Provided that no Amendment which may be made prior to the Year One thousand eight hundred and eight shall in any Manner affect the first and fourth Clauses in the Ninth Section of the first Article; and that no State, without its Consent, shall be deprived of its equal Suffrage in the Senate.

Article. VI.

All Debts contracted and Engagements entered into, before the Adoption of this Constitution, shall be as valid against the United States under this Constitution, as under the Confederation.

This Constitution, and the Laws of the United States which shall be made in Pursuance thereof; and all Treaties made, or which shall be made, under the Authority of the United States, shall be the supreme Law of the Land; and the Judges in every State shall be bound thereby, any Thing in the Constitution or Laws of any State to the Contrary notwithstanding.

The Senators and Representatives before mentioned, and the Members of the several State Legislatures, and all executive and judicial Officers, both of the United States and of the several States, shall be bound by Oath or Affirmation, to support this Constitution; but no religious Test shall ever be required as a Qualification to any Office or public Trust under the United States.

Article. VII.

The ratification of the Conventions of nine States, shall be sufficient for the Establishment of this Constitution between the States so ratifying the Same.

Done in convention by the unanimous consent of the states present the seventeenth day of September in the year of our Lord one thousand seven hundred and eighty seven and of the independence of the United

States of America the twelfth. In witness whereof We have hereunto subscribed our Names,

G. Washington-Presidt. and deputy from Virginia
New Hampshire: John Langdon, Nicholas Gilman
Massachusetts: Nathaniel Gorham, Rufus King
Connecticut: Wm: Saml. Johnson, Roger Sherman
New York: Alexander Hamilton
New Jersey: Wil: Livingston, David Brearly, Wm. Paterson, Jona: Dayton
Pennsylvania: B. Franklin, Thomas Mifflin, Robt. Morris, Geo. Clymer, Thos. FitzSimons, Jared Ingersoll, James Wilson, Gouv Morris
Delaware: Geo: Read, Gunning Bedford jun, John Dickinson, Richard Bassett, Jaco: Broom
Maryland: James McHenry, Dan of St Thos. Jenifer, Danl Carroll
Virginia: John Blair–, James Madison Jr.
North Carolina: Wm. Blount, Richd. Dobbs Spaight, Hu Williamson
South Carolina: J. Rutledge, Charles Cotesworth Pinckney, Charles Pinckney, Pierce Butler
Georgia: William Few, Abr Baldwin

Bill of Rights

First Amendment

(ratified December 15, 1791)

Congress shall make no law respecting an establishment of religion, or prohibiting the free exercise thereof; or abridging the freedom of speech, or of the press; or the right of the people peaceably to assemble, and to petition the Government for a redress of grievances.

Second Amendment

(ratified December 15, 1791)

A well regulated Militia, being necessary to the security of a free State, the right of the people to keep and bear Arms shall not be infringed.

Third Amendment

(ratified December 15, 1791)

No Soldier shall, in time of peace be quartered in any house, without the consent of the Owner, nor in time of war, but in a manner to be prescribed by law.

Fourth Amendment

(ratified December 15, 1791)

The right of the people to be secure in their persons, houses, papers, and effects, against unreasonable searches and seizures, shall not be violated, and no Warrants shall issue, but upon probable cause, supported by Oath or affirmation, and particularly describing the place to be searched, and the persons or things to be seized.

Fifth Amendment

(ratified December 15, 1791)

No person shall be held to answer for a capital, or otherwise infamous crime, unless on a presentment or indictment of a Grand Jury, except in cases arising in the land or naval forces, or in the Militia, when in actual service in time of War or public danger; nor shall any person be subject for the same offence to be twice put in jeopardy of life or limb; nor shall be compelled in any criminal case to be a witness against himself, nor be deprived of life, liberty, or property, without due process of law; nor shall private property be taken for public use, without just compensation.

Sixth Amendment

(ratified December 15, 1791)

In all criminal prosecutions, the accused shall enjoy the right to a speedy and public trial, by an impartial jury of the State and district wherein the crime shall have been committed, which district shall have been previously ascertained by law, and to be informed of the nature and cause of the accusation; to be confronted with the witnesses against him; to have compulsory process for obtaining witnesses in his favor, and to have the Assistance of Counsel for his defense.

Seventh Amendment

(ratified December 15, 1791)

In Suits at common law, where the value in controversy shall exceed twenty dollars, the right of trial by jury shall be preserved, and no fact tried by a jury, shall be otherwise re-examined in any Court of the United States, than according to the rules of the common law.

Eighth Amendment

(ratified December 15, 1791)

Excessive bail shall not be required, nor excessive fines imposed, nor cruel and unusual punishments inflicted.

Ninth Amendment

(ratified December 15, 1791)

The enumeration in the Constitution, of certain rights, shall not be construed to deny or disparage others retained by the people.

Tenth Amendment

(ratified December 15, 1791)

The powers not delegated to the United States by the Constitution, nor prohibited by it to the States, are reserved to the States respectively, or to the people.

Eleventh Amendment

Passed by Congress March 4, 1794. Ratified February 7, 1795.

Note: Article III, section 2, of the Constitution was modified by amendment 11.

The Judicial power of the United States shall not be construed to extend to any suit in law or equity, commenced or prosecuted against one of the United States by Citizens of another State, or by Citizens or Subjects of any Foreign State.

Twelfth Amendment

Passed by Congress December 9, 1803. Ratified June 15, 1804.

Note: A portion of Article II, section 1 of the Constitution was superseded by the 12th amendment.

The Electors shall meet in their respective states and vote by ballot for President and Vice-President, one of whom, at least, shall not be an inhabitant of the same state with themselves; they shall name in their ballots the person voted for as President, and in distinct ballots the person voted for as Vice-President, and they shall make distinct lists of all persons voted for as President, and of all persons voted for as Vice-President, and of the number of votes for each, which lists they shall sign and certify, and transmit sealed to the seat of the government of the United States, directed to the President of the Senate; — the President of the Senate shall, in the presence of the Senate and House of Representatives, open all the certificates and the votes shall then be counted; — The person having the greatest number of votes for President, shall be the President, if such number be a majority of the whole number of Electors appointed; and if no person have such majority, then from the persons having the highest numbers not exceeding three on the list of those voted for as President, the House of Representatives shall choose immediately, by ballot, the President. But in choosing the President, the votes shall be taken by states, the representation from each state having one vote; a quorum for this purpose shall consist of a member or members from two-thirds of the states, and a majority of all the states shall be necessary to a choice. [And if the House of Representatives shall not choose a President whenever the right of choice shall devolve upon them, before the fourth day of March next following, then the Vice-President shall act as President, as in case of the death or other constitutional disability of the President. –]* The person having the greatest number of votes as Vice-President, shall be the Vice-President, if such number be a majority of the whole number of Electors appointed, and if no person have a majority, then from the two highest numbers on the list, the Senate shall choose the Vice-President; a quorum for the purpose shall consist of two-thirds of the whole number of Senators, and a majority of the whole number shall be necessary to a choice. But no person constitutionally ineligible to the office of President shall be eligible to that of Vice-President of the United States. *Superseded by section 3 of the 20th amendment.

Thirteenth Amendment

Passed by Congress January 31, 1865. Ratified December 6, 1865.

Note: A portion of Article IV, section 2, of the Constitution was superseded by the 13th amendment.

Section 1.

Neither slavery nor involuntary servitude, except as a punishment for crime whereof the party shall have been duly convicted, shall exist within the United States, or any place subject to their jurisdiction.

Section 2.

Congress shall have power to enforce this article by appropriate legislation.

Fourteenth Amendment

Passed by Congress June 13, 1866. Ratified July 9, 1868.

Note: Article I, section 2, of the Constitution was modified by section 2 of the 14th amendment.

Section 1.

All persons born or naturalized in the United States, and subject to the jurisdiction thereof, are citizens of the United States and of the State wherein they reside. No State shall make or enforce any law which shall abridge the privileges or immunities of citizens of the United States; nor shall any State deprive any person of life, liberty, or property, without due process of law; nor deny to any person within its jurisdiction the equal protection of the laws.

Section 2.

Representatives shall be apportioned among the several States according to their respective numbers, counting the whole number of persons in each State, excluding Indians not taxed. But when the right to vote at any election for the choice of electors for President and Vice-President of the United States, Representatives in Congress, the Executive and Judicial officers of a State, or the members of the Legislature thereof, is denied to any of the male inhabitants of such State, being twenty-one years of age,* and citizens of the United States, or in any way abridged, except for participation in rebellion, or other crime, the basis of representation therein shall be reduced in the proportion which the number of such male citizens shall bear to the whole number of male citizens twenty-one years of age in such State.

Section 3.

No person shall be a Senator or Representative in Congress, or elector of President and Vice-President, or hold any office, civil or military, under the United States, or under any State, who, having previously taken an oath, as a member of Congress, or as an officer of the United States, or as a member of any State legislature, or as an executive or judicial officer of any State, to support the Constitution of the United States, shall have engaged in insurrection or rebellion against the same, or given aid or comfort to the enemies thereof. But Congress may by a vote of two-thirds of each House, remove such disability.

Section 4.

The validity of the public debt of the United States, authorized by law, including debts incurred for payment of pensions and bounties for services in suppressing insurrection or rebellion, shall not be questioned. But neither the United States nor any State shall assume or pay any debt or obligation incurred in aid of insurrection or rebellion against the United States, or any claim for the loss or emancipation of any slave; but all such debts, obligations and claims shall be held illegal and void.

Section 5.

The Congress shall have the power to enforce, by appropriate legislation, the provisions of this article.

*Changed by section 1 of the 26th amendment.

Fifteenth Amendment

Passed by Congress February 26, 1869. Ratified February 3, 1870.

Section 1.

The right of citizens of the United States to vote shall not be denied or abridged by the United States or by any State on account of race, color, or previous condition of servitude.

Section 2.

The Congress shall have the power to enforce this article by appropriate legislation.

Sixteenth Amendment

Passed by Congress July 2, 1909. Ratified February 3, 1913.

Note: Article I, section 9, of the Constitution was modified by amendment 16.

The Congress shall have power to lay and collect taxes on incomes, from whatever source derived, without apportionment among the several States, and without regard to any census or enumeration.

Seventeenth Amendment

Passed by Congress May 13, 1912. Ratified April 8, 1913.

Note: Article I, section 3, of the Constitution was modified by the 17th amendment.

The Senate of the United States shall be composed of two Senators from each State, elected by the people thereof, for six years; and each Senator shall have one vote. The electors in each State shall have the qualifications requisite for electors of the most numerous branch of the State legislatures.

When vacancies happen in the representation of any State in the Senate, the executive authority of such State shall issue writs of election to fill such vacancies: Provided, That the legislature of any State may empower the executive thereof to make temporary appointments until the people fill the vacancies by election as the legislature may direct.

This amendment shall not be so construed as to affect the election or term of any Senator chosen before it becomes valid as part of the Constitution.

Eighteenth Amendment

Passed by Congress December 18, 1917. Ratified January 16, 1919. Repealed by amendment 21.

Section 1.

After one year from the ratification of this article the manufacture, sale, or transportation of intoxicating liquors within, the importation thereof into, or the exportation thereof from the United States and all territory subject to the jurisdiction thereof for beverage purposes is hereby prohibited.

Section 2.
The Congress and the several States shall have concurrent power to enforce this article by appropriate legislation.

Section 3.
This article shall be inoperative unless it shall have been ratified as an amendment to the Constitution by the legislatures of the several States, as provided in the Constitution, within seven years from the date of the submission hereof to the States by the Congress.

Nineteenth Amendment
Passed by Congress June 4, 1919. Ratified August 18, 1920.

The right of citizens of the United States to vote shall not be denied or abridged by the United States or by any State on account of sex.
Congress shall have power to enforce this article by appropriate legislation.

Twentieth Amendment
Passed by Congress March 2, 1932. Ratified January 23, 1933.

Note: Article I, section 4, of the Constitution was modified by section 2 of this amendment. In addition, a portion of the 12th amendment was superseded by section 3.

Section 1.
The terms of the President and the Vice President shall end at noon on the 20th day of January, and the terms of Senators and Representatives at noon on the 3d day of January, of the years in which such terms

would have ended if this article had not been ratified; and the terms of their successors shall then begin.

Section 2.

The Congress shall assemble at least once in every year, and such meeting shall begin at noon on the 3d day of January, unless they shall by law appoint a different day.

Section 3.

If, at the time fixed for the beginning of the term of the President, the President elect shall have died, the Vice President elect shall become President. If a President shall not have been chosen before the time fixed for the beginning of his term, or if the President elect shall have failed to qualify, then the Vice President elect shall act as President until a President shall have qualified; and the Congress may by law provide for the case wherein neither a President elect nor a Vice President elect shall have qualified, declaring who shall then act as President, or the manner in which one who is to act shall be selected, and such person shall act accordingly until a President or Vice President shall have qualified.

Section 4.

The Congress may by law provide for the case of the death of any of the persons from whom the House of Representatives may choose a President whenever the right of choice shall have devolved upon them, and for the case of the death of any of the persons from whom the Senate may choose a Vice President whenever the right of choice shall have devolved upon them.

Section 5.

Sections 1 and 2 shall take effect on the 15th day of October following the ratification of this article.

Section 6.

This article shall be inoperative unless it shall have been ratified as an amendment to the Constitution by the legislatures of three-fourths of the several States within seven years from the date of its submission.

Twenty-First Amendment

Passed by Congress February 20, 1933. Ratified December 5, 1933.

Section 1.

The eighteenth article of amendment to the Constitution of the United States is hereby repealed.

Section 2.

The transportation or importation into any State, Territory, or possession of the United States for delivery or use therein of intoxicating liquors, in violation of the laws thereof, is hereby prohibited.

Section 3.

This article shall be inoperative unless it shall have been ratified as an amendment to the Constitution by conventions in the several States, as provided in the Constitution, within seven years from the date of the submission hereof to the States by the Congress.

Twenty-Second Amendment

Passed by Congress March 21, 1947. Ratified February 27, 1951.

Section 1.

No person shall be elected to the office of the President more than twice, and no person who has held the office of President, or acted as President, for more than two years of a term to which some other person was elected President shall be elected to the office of the President more than once. But this Article shall not apply to any person holding the office of President when this Article was proposed by the Congress, and shall not prevent any person who may be holding the office of President, or acting as President, during the term within which this Article becomes operative from holding the office of President or acting as President during the remainder of such term.

Section 2.

This article shall be inoperative unless it shall have been ratified as an amendment to the Constitution by the legislatures of three-fourths of the several States within seven years from the date of its submission to the States by the Congress.

Twenty-Third Amendment

Passed by Congress June 16, 1960. Ratified March 29, 1961.

Section 1.

The District constituting the seat of Government of the United States shall appoint in such manner as the Congress may direct:

A number of electors of President and Vice President equal to the whole number of Senators and Representatives in Congress to which the District would be entitled if it were a State, but in no event more than the least populous State; they shall be in addition to those appointed by the States, but they shall be considered, for the purposes of the election of President and Vice President, to be electors appointed by a State; and they shall meet in the District and perform such duties as provided by the twelfth article of amendment.

Section 2.
The Congress shall have power to enforce this article by appropriate legislation.

Twenty-Fourth Amendment
Passed by Congress August 27, 1962. Ratified January 23, 1964.

Section 1.
The right of citizens of the United States to vote in any primary or other election for President or Vice President, for electors for President or Vice President, or for Senator or Representative in Congress, shall not be denied or abridged by the United States or any State by reason of failure to pay any poll tax or other tax.

Section 2.
The Congress shall have power to enforce this article by appropriate legislation.

Twenty-Fifth Amendment

Passed by Congress July 6, 1965. Ratified February 10, 1967.

Note: Article II, section 1, of the Constitution was affected by the 25th amendment.

Section 1.

In case of the removal of the President from office or of his death or resignation, the Vice President shall become President.

Section 2.

Whenever there is a vacancy in the office of the Vice President, the President shall nominate a Vice President who shall take office upon confirmation by a majority vote of both Houses of Congress.

Section 3.

Whenever the President transmits to the President pro tempore of the Senate and the Speaker of the House of Representatives his written declaration that he is unable to discharge the powers and duties of his office, and until he transmits to them a written declaration to the contrary, such powers and duties shall be discharged by the Vice President as Acting President.

Section 4.

Whenever the Vice President and a majority of either the principal officers of the executive departments or of such other body as Congress may by law provide, transmit to the President pro tempore of the Senate and the Speaker of the House of Representatives their written declaration that the President is unable to discharge the powers and duties of his office, the Vice President shall immediately assume the powers and duties of the office as Acting President.

Thereafter, when the President transmits to the President pro tempore of the Senate and the Speaker of the House of Representatives his written declaration that no inability exists, he shall resume the powers and duties of his office unless the Vice President and a majority of either the principal officers of the executive department or of such other body as Congress may by law provide, transmit within four days to the President pro tempore of the Senate and the Speaker of the House of Representatives their written declaration that the President is unable to discharge the powers and duties of his office. Thereupon Congress shall decide the issue, assembling within forty-eight hours for that purpose if not in session. If the Congress, within twenty-one days after receipt of the latter written declaration, or, if Congress is not in session, within twenty-one days after Congress is required to assemble, determines by two-thirds vote of both Houses that the President is unable to discharge the powers and duties of his office, the Vice President shall continue to discharge the same as Acting President; otherwise, the President shall resume the powers and duties of his office.

Twenty-Sixth Amendment

Passed by Congress March 23, 1971. Ratified July 1, 1971.

Note: Amendment 14, section 2, of the Constitution was modified by section 1 of the 26th amendment.

Section 1.
The right of citizens of the United States, who are eighteen years of age or older, to vote shall not be denied or abridged by the United States or by any State on account of age.

Section 2.
The Congress shall have power to enforce this article by appropriate legislation.

Twenty-Seventh Amendment
Originally proposed Sept. 25, 1789. Ratified May 7, 1992.
No law, varying the compensation for the services of the Senators and Representatives, shall take effect, until an election of Representatives shall have intervened.

Made in United States
North Haven, CT
10 September 2025

72379141R00114